Look Who's Morphing

LOOK WHO'S MORPHING

Tom Cho

Arsenal Pulp Press  Vancouver

First North American and UK edition: 2014

Published originally in Australia and New Zealand by Giramondo Publishing

ARSENAL PULP PRESS
Suite 202–211 East Georgia St.
Vancouver, BC V6A 1Z6
Canada
arsenalpulp.com

This is a work of fiction. Any resemblance of characters to persons either living or deceased is purely coincidental.

Book design: Gerilee McBride
Cover image: Owen Leong, *Tom*, 2009 © Owen Leong / SODRAC (2013).
owenleong.com

Printed and bound in Canada

Library and Archives Canada Cataloguing in Publication

Cho, Tom, author
    Look who's morphing / Tom Cho. —First North American and UK edition.

Short stories.
Originally published: Artarmon, N.S.W. : Giramondo Publishing, 2009.
Issued in print and electronic formats.
ISBN 978-1-55152-538-9 (pbk.).—ISBN 978-1-55152-539-6 (epub)

    I. Title.

PR9619.4.C46L66 2014   823'.92   C2014-901484-8
                                               C2014-901485-6

This book is dedicated to the memory of my father.

CONTENTS

9 *Dirty Dancing*

15 *Suitmation*

19 *The Exorcist*

25 *Dinner with My Brother*

27 *Dinner with My Grandmother*

31 *Dinner with Auntie Ling and Uncle Wang*

35 *The Sound of Music*

41 *Learning English*

43 *Today on Dr. Phil*

49 *Chinese Whispers*

53 *A Counting Rhyme*

55 *The Bodyguard*

63 *AIYO!!! An Evil Group of Ninjas is Entering and Destroying a Call Centre!!!*

65 *I, Robot*

73 *My Life in China*

75 *Pinocchio*

85 *Look Who's Morphing*

97 *Cock Rock*

125 *Acknowledgments*

DIRTY DANCING

⋮
▼

This is the summer of 1963 and everybody is calling me "Baby." I am at a resort with my Auntie Feng and Uncle Stan for a holiday. The resort is on a small island that is located ten miles off the coast of North Devon where the Atlantic meets the Bristol Channel. My auntie and uncle think the resort is very exciting and they soon get involved in all the resort activities—golf, macramé, etc. Me, I think the only moderately interesting thing about the resort is Johnny Castle. Johnny is a dance instructor at the resort and he has a very nice body. As it turns out, Johnny ends up teaching me the mambo in preparation for a dance performance together and so we start spending a lot of time with one another. In fact, one night, Johnny and I find ourselves alone in his cabin. At first, we are just talking about our favourite '80s television shows and pop songs. But there is something in the way that discussions about popular culture can bring people together and hence our conversation soon leads to Johnny and me having sex. The thing is, while Johnny looks very nice and all, I do not really feel very "in the moment." In fact, as Johnny is panting and thrusting, I feel very detached from the experience. It is like I am a bystander, looking on as someone else is having sex with Johnny. And that someone else is a Caucasian man with a moustache. This man is tall and very well-built. He is wearing a leather cap and leather chaps. His name? Bruce. As Bruce reaches for Johnny's wrists, I take the opportunity to watch him. I find myself admiring the sheer physical power of Bruce's masculinity. And Bruce is so confident when it comes to sex. He doesn't say anything; he just pushes Johnny's face into the pillow. In the end, I watch as Bruce and Johnny spend all night having the hottest sex you can imagine.

The next morning, Bruce and Johnny get out of bed. They are feeling tired from a lack of sleep from the night before, but they are also pleased about the sex that they have had and the fact that they have gotten together. They hope that everyone else is going to be pleased that they are now a couple. But it turns out that Auntie Feng is not pleased about them being together at all and I look on as she forbids Bruce from seeing Johnny. Auntie Feng tells Bruce that he and Johnny need to have a relationship that is more like the one she has with Uncle Stan. Uncle Stan first met Auntie Feng when he went on a business trip to Shanghai in 1968. Uncle Stan then brought Auntie Feng over to Australia to be his wife. Theirs is a marriage of convenience. She has a type of green algae growing on her and he has a rare type of fungus growing on him, such that her green algae receives water and nutrient salts from his fungus, and in turn his fungus gains nutrients synthesised from her green algae. Bruce tells Auntie Feng that he could never have a relationship as perfect as the one she and Uncle Stan have, but Auntie Feng still refuses to give him and Johnny her approval. Thus, over the next few days, things are not looking so good for Bruce and Johnny. But, a few nights later in Johnny's cabin, there is a breakthrough. Bruce is right in the middle of having sex with Johnny when he discovers that Johnny has a special kind of intracellular methane-oxidizing bacteria in his hair and Bruce's own body produces a particular kind of enzyme, such that Johnny's bacteria is able to convert methane to a form that Bruce can use for nutrition, and in turn Bruce's enzyme protects Johnny from the harmful hydrogen peroxide that is a byproduct of Johnny's sulphur metabolizing process. So Bruce and Johnny talk over the situation with me and then the three of us go to see Auntie Feng, and Bruce and Johnny show her Johnny's bacteria and Bruce's enzyme, and then I watch as Johnny says to Auntie Feng "No one puts Baby in a corner," and he performs a big raunchy dance number with Bruce after he says it and everyone else at the resort joins in and starts dancing in a raunchy way too.

Auntie Feng has no comeback for all of this. As a result, she has no choice but to give Johnny and Bruce her blessing.

After the resort's end-of-season show, my holiday comes to a close. On my last morning at the resort, I wake up early to pack my luggage and then I run over to Johnny's cabin. I watch as Bruce and Johnny load their belongings into Johnny's black Chevy. After the car is loaded and ready to go, Bruce and Johnny turn to me to say goodbye. Johnny gives me a hug and he whispers, "I'll see ya." He gets into the Chevy and starts the engine. Bruce and I turn to each other. We do not say anything for a moment. I say, "I guess we surprised everybody." He smiles at me and says, "I guess we did." As we embrace, I feel his muscular body against me. We promise that we will keep in touch. Bruce then gets into the Chevy, and I stand and watch as the Chevy disappears into the distance. Eventually, I turn away from the road. I begin walking back to my cabin where I know Auntie Feng and Uncle Stan are waiting for me. Soon, Auntie Feng and Uncle Stan will be heading back to their home in Hobart. Me, I am due to catch a plane back to Melbourne.

My parents meet me at Melbourne Airport. They are very happy to see me. As always, they literally pass me around like I am a baby. My mother holds me in her arms and exclaims over my fingers and toes and then she passes me to my father. As my father cradles me, he starts cooing to me in baby-talk. He says to me, "What's your name, hmmm? What's your name? Can you say your name?" and then he tickles my foot. Given the fact that I am known as "Baby," none of this is surprising. Furthermore, my parents have been treating me like this for years and I have never felt that it will ever change. But, this time, it annoys me more than usual. I take a deep breath and I tell my parents that I am not a baby. But my mother only pokes at my belly button and tells me that I am a little Buddha. My father then holds me up in the air and proclaims that I will grow up to be prosperous and successful. I am unsure about what to do. The placating part of me tells me to keep the peace and go along with everything, the logical part of me tells me that being prosperous and successful would be very nice, the fearful part of me tells me that I need to be held by my father, and the newer part of me—the part that learned dancing at the resort—tells me that dancing, like pop culture discussions, brings people together. In the end, the part of me that learned dancing at the resort wins out, and so I jump out of my father's arms and I say to my parents, "No one puts Baby in a corner," and I perform a big raunchy dance number after I say it and everyone else at the airport joins in and starts dancing in a raunchy way too.

My parents have no comeback for all of this. As a result, they have no choice but to come to terms with the fact that I am an adult.

SUITMATION

Suitmation is a special-effects technique that involves the use of an actor in a costumed suit.

The most famous examples of suitmation are in the *Godzilla* films. Over the years, various suitmation actors have played Godzilla.

The early days of suitmation were difficult for suitmation actors. The suits, which were typically made of foam latex, were heavy and uncomfortable. Haruo Nakajima, who played Godzilla until 1973, lost twenty kilograms during the filming of the original 1954 *Godzilla* film.

These days, the suits are much more comfortable, and are more likely to depict humans than monsters. They are also far more realistic and much cheaper to produce. All of this has allowed suitmation to move beyond film-making and within the reach of the everyday consumer.

As a result, suitmation has changed our society. Most of the people I know own at least one suitmation suit. Furthermore, most of these people wear a suitmation suit every day.

My brother Hank bought me my first suit when I was fifteen. I had always been a big Suzi Quatro fan so I ended up getting a Suzi Quatro suit.

We took the suit home. I wanted to try it on straight away so I took the suit out of its wrapping. It included Suzi's classic leather jumpsuit and snakeskin platform boots. The headpiece also perfectly replicated Suzi's face and hairstyle from 1973.

I closed my eyes and smelled the black leather. At that point, I couldn't wait any longer so I stepped into my Suzi Quatro suit and pulled it over my body. Hank helped me with the headpiece and he showed me how to zip the whole suit up. We walked to my mother's bedroom where there was a full-length mirror. I went over to the mirror, looked at myself, and felt elated to see that Suzi Quatro was staring back at me elatedly.

My Uncle Wang's favourite suit is his Tony Danza suit. Everyone says that he looks exactly like Tony Danza. In fact, Uncle Wang once confided to me that he likes to look at himself in his bathroom mirror and say to his reflection: "Hey! Aren't you that guy who was in that show *Who's the Boss?*"

Even my mother owns a suit. I remember visiting her on Christmas Day five years ago. I strutted up to her house in my Suzi Quatro suit and rang the doorbell. She opened her front door and there was Olivia Newton-John.

As much as I like suitmation, I have come to realize that I have mixed feelings about its popularity. These days, everyone wears suits; everyone is a celebrity.

As a result, I don't know who my friends are any more. They are all movie stars and pop stars. And then there is the situation with my mother. She has been a lot happier since she became Olivia Newton-John. In fact, she recently started telling all of her friends that Olivia Newton-John has a timeless appeal. My mother and I have never been that close and now

I wonder whether we ever will be. I have this feeling that she will be Olivia Newton-John for the rest of her life.

I have one more thing to say, and that is that something awful happened last week:

My Auntie Wei's hot bread shop was robbed. Auntie Wei had set up the shop in the suburb of Footscray over twenty years ago. She has always loved her shop and had never been robbed until last week.

The shop was robbed just after the lunchtime rush, when the very last pork bun had been sold. The two perpetrators looked just like Daniel and Mr Miyagi from the first three *Karate Kid* films. They stole more than $2,000 in cash. They also took the bread slicer and the pie oven. Worse still, they tied up Auntie Wei, who looked just like Angela Lansbury in *Murder, She Wrote*.

Auntie Wei says that now she is going to sell her shop.

THE EXORCIST

▼

There are some blood-red credits on a black background and then the opening scene appears and this shows Auntie Wei and me, drinking beers in a crowded bar in the city. Auntie Wei is only on her first beer but her face is already flushed. She looks deep into my eyes and tells me that she has a head for business and a body for sin, just like Melanie Griffith's character in the film *Working Girl*. The thing is, although I am not that close to Auntie Wei, I feel that what she has said is not the truth at all. I even feel like telling Auntie Wei how things really are, which would involve saying "Actually, Auntie, you have a head for surly customer service and a body for lactose intolerance," but instead I buy her another beer. Half an hour later, we are at a novelty store on Swanston Street and Auntie Wei is buying one of those aprons that has fake plastic breasts attached, and it is then that I realize that you can take the auntie out of China but you can't take the alcohol intolerance out of the auntie. I warn my auntie that the breasts on the apron will look very fake on her because the breasts look so obviously made out of plastic. However, Auntie Wei is more concerned that the breasts on the apron will look very fake on her because they are of Caucasian skin tone. At any rate, Auntie Wei insists on wearing the breast apron straight away. As we walk to Flinders Street station to catch the train back to my place, I notice that Auntie Wei's wearing of the breast apron is causing other people to see her differently. It is as if other people see her as someone else. I eventually notice that Auntie Wei is not quite acting like herself anyway. At first, I think that this is a classic case of "clothes make the man, but aprons with fake plastic breasts make you act a little differently," but I soon realize that it all goes much further than this. In fact, by the time we have arrived at my place, things have become much stranger and Auntie Wei's head is spinning around and around the full 360 degrees and she is projectile vomiting all over my lounge room. She vomits all over the handmade rug and all over the leather three-seater sofa and all over the walls. This change in Auntie Wei's manner disturbs me. Over the years, I have never felt that I really knew Auntie Wei and it seems to me that her behaviour is only proving this point. Then again, I am aware that she and I have rarely made the effort to get to know each other more deeply. I take a deep breath and I think about raising all of this with Auntie Wei but her eyes glow red and she says to me in a deep voice: "We hate you. Fuck you, fuck you, fuck you, fuck you, fuck you, fuck you, fuck you, fuck you, fuck you, fuck you, fuck you, fuck you, fuck you, fuck you, fuck you, fuck you, fuck you, we hate you. Oh yes, we hate you." I briefly wonder why Auntie Wei has started using the royal "we" but I soon realize that she in fact has a head for swearing and a body for demonic possession. At first, this realization gives me a sense of relief: since demonic possession means that Auntie Wei has, in a sense, become someone else, perhaps this means that I do know my auntie better than I had thought. It also occurs to me that I must rescue Auntie Wei from her demonic possession. I say, "Who are you and what have you done with the real Auntie Wei?" but Auntie Wei only laughs and lies back on the vomit-splattered couch. Her body soon starts levitating into the air. She also starts talking in different voices: at first, a guttural-sounding swearing voice, then a childlike pleading voice, then a deep and booming voice talking in biblical language, and even a puppy-like voice of barking and growling but then whining and whimpering. Then Auntie Wei shocks me by suddenly talking in a voice that sounds just like mine. In fact, she soon begins to speak in various voices of mine: at first a softly spoken voice greeting me hello, then a mumbling voice making awkward small talk, then a soothing and fatherly voice offering me protection, and even a confident and businesslike voice quoting from successful arts funding applications that I have written. I spend a little while listening to these and other voices of myself as spoken by Auntie Wei. I also begin wondering if—demonic possession aside—my auntie may have the capacity to understand me far better than I ever thought. However, when Auntie Wei goes on to say, "As indicated by the project timeline (see *Timing* section below), by the time the proposed funded period would commence, work on the project will be more advanced and I would then be in a position to more significantly benefit from Australia Council funding," I realize that her demonic possession has gone too far and that it must be stopped. I run to the study and get a crucifix from my bottom desk drawer. I run back into the lounge room, yell at my auntie "I banish you forever, you devil!" and hold the crucifix up to her. But Auntie Wei only grabs the crucifix from me and begins masturbating with it and as she rubs it against her crotch she declares, "My work on this collection demonstrates that I am capable of: 1) producing a body of short works that are thematically linked, and 2) working productively with the assistance of arts funding support." As she begins saying this, a new realization occurs to me: in order to remove the demon from Auntie Wei, the breast apron must be removed from her body. As I know that this is a job that must be left to the experts, I call an ambulance. Around ten minutes later, an ambulance arrives. The paramedics are very professional and they manage to grab hold of Auntie Wei and put her into the ambulance as she vomits and curses and masturbates and continues to quote from my successful arts funding applications. Auntie Wei is taken to The Royal Women's Hospital in the ambulance while I follow behind in my car. She is wheeled into the operating theatre straight away while I sit in the waiting room. It takes a team of twelve surgeons almost fifteen hours to remove the breast apron from Auntie Wei but, once they do, the demon is banished from her body. I spend the night at the hospital pacing the corridor and reading tabloid magazines and I wait and wait until the doctors tell me that it is okay for Auntie Wei to spend a brief amount of time with visitors. I go to Auntie Wei's room and see her lying on the bed, tired but awake. It turns out that Auntie Wei has no memory of what has happened. She says to me, "I hope I didn't cause you too much trouble." I pause for a moment and then I break the awkward silence by replying "Actually, Auntie, I have always felt that you are one of my favourite relatives and I respect you very much and, although we have never known each other very well, I just want you to know how important you are to me," and I hold her hand and we smile at each other, and thus a potentially problematic situation diffuses into a nice family moment—a family moment that makes me feel much closer to Auntie Wei than usual. I stay at her bedside and we talk for a while longer. However, after about fifteen minutes, I can see that Auntie Wei is becoming tired. I hug her and I promise her that I will be back to visit tomorrow. As I leave the room, I look at her for a moment. She is smiling at me. At the entrance to the hospital, I pause at the top of the stairs. I have a solemn look on my face. I then turn away from the hospital and walk into the distance. The music of "Tubular Bells" is playing and then there's the blood-red title on a black background that appears and this closing title says: *"THE EXORCIST."*

DINNER
WITH MY BROTHER

▼

Went to Hank's new townhouse for dinner last night. Hank was really happy to see me. He proudly gave me a tour of his ultra-modern house and then he cooked up a fine dinner— sweet and sour pork using the traditional recipe passed down from generation to generation within our family. After dinner, we got into a discussion re: our Chinese names and their meanings. We both agreed that the meaning of a person's name seems to be quite significant in Chinese culture. Told Hank that Dad chose my Chinese name but that I have never been happy with its meaning. My Chinese name—which my mother has told me is a very pretty name—apparently means "I will skip and pick clover from lush fields." Hate it hate it hate it. Told Hank that our Auntie Wei doesn't like the meaning of her Chinese name either. Her name means "A very nice and intact hymen." Hank said he thought we were both being too critical. But he is only saying that because his Chinese name means "A very canny and all-powerful emperor with a loyal army of millions." I know our grandfather would side with Hank, but that's because Grandfather's name means "Not only clever and lucky, but strong, handsome and patriotic too." But there was one thing Hank and I agreed on. We started reminiscing about the time when our cousin, Summer Lotus, had her first child and our grandmother had the duty of picking the baby's Chinese name. I remember very clearly that afternoon at The Royal

Women's Hospital. The entire family was gathered at Summer Lotus's bedside. Summer Lotus held up the newborn child and showed him to everyone present before placing him into the arms of our grandmother. Our grandmother took one look at the baby and chose a name that meant "Middle management." Now, almost two years later, Hank and I agreed that that name was a strange choice. Hank then recounted the story of Dad's arrival in Australia after the long boat trip from China. Dad arrived in Brisbane and was asked by immigration officials to change his name to a "roughly equivalent" anglicized name. Dad refused because there was no anglicized name that could approximate the meaning of his Chinese name, which roughly translates to "Mr Amazing." There was apparently a big argument but Dad won. Hearing that story made me tell Hank about something that Dad once told me about my Chinese name. About ten years ago, when I first found out that I had a Chinese name, I asked Dad why he had chosen that name for me. Dad had replied that when a parent names a child, it expresses a wish that the parent has for their child. I then confessed to Hank my long-standing belief that if I could have any name at all, it would be "Marlon Brando." Told him I thought it was a name that expressed my own wishes for myself. Hank then declared to me that if he could have any name it would be "Indiana Jones." He said it was because of the marketing slogan for the Indiana Jones films. He quoted the slogan to me: "If 'adventure' has a name, it must be 'Indiana Jones.'" I told Hank: "If 'patchy employment history' has a name, then that name must be 'Tom Cho.'" Hank agreed.

DINNER WITH MY GRANDMOTHER

I am at my grandmother's house for dinner. I like visiting my grandmother. Although we do not know very much about each other and we do not even have proficiency in the same language, I enjoy being with her and being in her house. My grandmother lives in a two-storey house. It is filled with all sorts of objects and memorabilia from China. Years ago, as a child, I helped my family sort through everything that my grandmother had shipped from China to Australia. This collection is quite sizeable. She has traditional Chinese costumes that she bought many years ago, genuine jade jewellery from China that she inherited from her mother, Chinese posters that were given to her by friends in China, corpses of Chinese people that she stole from cemeteries in Beijing, and more.

My grandmother serves up the dinner in her dining room. These days, although she is becoming frail, she still insists on cooking dinner without any assistance. Tonight, she has cooked lemon chicken using the traditional recipe that has been passed down from generation to generation within our family. I smile at my grandmother and I gesture at the food as I compliment her on her cooking. My grandmother does not know many English words so she replies: "*Mon chien a été vacciné contre la rage. On lui a ensuite fait une analyse de sang, avec un résultat satisfaisant. Mon animal ne réside pas en France. Il n'a donc pas besoin d'être tatoué.*"

An interesting thing about my grandmother is that she is called Bruce. Apparently, this is due to an incident that occurred when my grandfather first courted my grandmother. My grandparents initially met on a skiing holiday. There was nothing my grandparents loved more than skiing the slopes of Shanghai, and it was on these slopes that they first met and fell in love. My grandfather had boldly approached my grandmother at the chair lifts. He had asked her what her name was, and she had seductively asked him what he wanted it to be, and he had declared that he really wanted her name to be Bruce, and so now my grandmother has to answer to that name.

After we finish the meal, my grandmother brings out the brandy and cigars. My grandmother loves smoking cigars and wearing baggy tracksuits. The only time I ever smoke cigars and wear tracksuits is when I see my grandmother, although I did smoke cigarettes and wear tight jeans for many years. In 1981, when I was seven, I wrote a note for my mother to take to the corner store up the road. The note said: "I am at home with two broken legs. Obviously my mobility has been impaired and so I am sending my mother to the shops to buy cigarettes for me. Can I please have a carton of menthol lights?" Regular use of that same note and my mother's cooperation in the whole matter kept me in cigarettes until May 8, 1992, when I became old enough to buy my own cigarettes.

As always, after the brandy and cigars, my grandmother brings out her Cantonese language book and she spends an hour with me in Cantonese language instruction. We sit at her kitchen table and she opens the book to show me some new words that she would like me to learn. I always try hard at my

Cantonese lessons because it makes me happy when I please my grandmother. Unfortunately, Cantonese is a very difficult language to learn. One reason for its difficulty is that it is a tonal language. This can result in many problems because changing the tone of a word can completely alter that word's meaning. Thus, to a beginner, the word for "electronic mail-sorting machine" can sound very similar to the word for "compulsory jury duty," and the word for "it's not a cat" can sound very similar to the word for "the Norwegians." My grandmother shows me the word for "do pork and prawn really go together?" and also the word for "the projector has broken down and I am the repair man." I also learn about the necessary tonal changes to convert the word for "guess which house is mine?" to the word for "I smell burning."

Once my Cantonese lesson is over, it is time to go. I say goodbye to my grandmother and leave. Just as I am walking down her paved driveway, I hear her call out to me. I turn around. She is waving at me. She smiles at me and she says: "*Si vous avez besoin de viande, vous allez chez le boucher. Vous pouvez y acheter toutes sortes de viands et de volailles, et si vous avez envie de bon jambon, ou de pâté ou d'autres produits du porc, vous allez chez le charcutier.*"

DINNER WITH AUNTIE LING AND UNCLE WANG

I am going to my auntie and uncle's apartment for dinner. I like visiting Auntie Ling and Uncle Wang. They both love hosting visitors. Auntie Ling is also an outstanding cook and her dinners typically showcase the best of northern Chinese cuisine. Although their one-bedroom apartment is very small, it has quite a large kitchen. This kitchen has a neon sign on the wall that says "Oriental Gourmet Kitchen" and Auntie Ling likes to stand in the kitchen stirring food that is in bains-marie. She always makes Uncle Wang and me queue up so that she can serve us lemon chicken and sweet and sour pork. When I arrive at the house, dinner is served very quickly, as usual. A few minutes later, over dinner in the lounge room, Auntie Ling tells me that her life sometimes seems quite similar to a Hollywood movie. Auntie Ling and Uncle Wang lived in a remote village in the Gobi Desert until only a year ago, so I think it is interesting that she feels that her life has some similarities to a Hollywood movie. I ask her what kind of movie and she says any movie made by National Lampoon. Me, I think my life sometimes seems quite similar to a Dungeons & Dragons game—or various other role-playing games—but I decide to keep that thought to myself. Auntie Ling then explains to me that she watches *Star Trek* films when she wants escapism but when she wants reality she watches *National Lampoon* films. Uncle Wang suddenly says that he has been getting an intriguing dose of escapism lately by volunteering as a subject for neural interfacing research. He is required to go to a university lab three times a week and be wired directly to a computer. As Uncle Wang begins to explain this research to me, I smile at him. While Uncle Wang and I do not have any long and personal conversations, what we do have are our conversations about computers. Furthermore, I come from a family of high achievers so it seems quite fitting that my uncle would end up having a bi-directional interface between his central nervous system and a computer. But then Uncle Wang confesses that the computer he is being connected to is only a 386 DX/33 that runs Microsoft Word 5 so he finds it all a bit slow. Then Uncle Wang suddenly starts saying over and over:

```
// Copy text into clipboard
if (OpenClipboard(NULL))
{
     HANDLE hMem =
     ::GlobalAlloc(GMEM_MOVEABLE|GMEM_DDESHARE,
     strToLookup.GetLength()+1);
     if (!hMem) return;
     LPSTR lpStr = (LPSTR)::GlobalLock(hMem);
     strcpy(lpStr, strToLookup);
     ::GlobalUnlock(hMem);
     VERIFY(::SetClipboardData(CF_TEXT,hMem));
     ::CloseClipboard();
} else
{
     AfxMessageBox('Failed to open the
     clipboard!');
     return;
}
```

Auntie Ling and I are alarmed at this sudden change in Uncle Wang. However, I have a solid background in IT so I begin to repair Uncle Wang while Auntie Ling clears the table. I soon discover that those university researchers have done quite a little number on him. It actually takes me almost four hours to repair Uncle Wang, but the gist of the repairs can be summarized in the following *MacGyver*-style montage: Tom opening Uncle Wang's head / Tom using a soldering iron / Tom driving to a local computer store to get new parts / Tom cutting wires / Tom wiping sweat from his brow / Tom using a boot disk to start up his uncle / Tom de-bugging various C++ programs / Tom closing Uncle Wang's head. It is past midnight by the time I have finished and my auntie and uncle are very grateful. They thank me for my hard work. Auntie Ling hugs me and tells me that she is very proud of me. I turn to my uncle and we smile at each other. He and I agree that, next time I visit, we will have a long talk about the C++ bugs that the university researchers introduced into his central nervous system. He shakes my hand and then it is time for me to go. I say goodbye to my auntie and uncle and turn to leave. But, before I can leave, an army of orcs suddenly enters the house and attacks us. As this is a classic Dungeons & Dragons scenario, I know exactly what to do. I immediately cast a Fireball that kills the entire army. Then I turn to see if Uncle Wang and Auntie Ling are wounded. Uncle Wang is unharmed but Auntie Ling has lost a few Hit Points so before I leave I cure her with a Potion of Healing and then I thank her for a great dinner.

THE SOUND OF MUSIC

At first, all you can see are clouds, then an aerial view of mountains, then a green valley, and a lake, and suddenly an open grassy area, and then there's me, spinning around with my arms outstretched and I am singing—or, more specifically, I am thinking about singing. As usual, I have come to the hills to think. Today, among other topics, I have been thinking about singing. It's interesting, really, because my Auntie Ping loves singing. Just as I have a tendency to run to the hills and think, Auntie Ping has a tendency to begin spontaneously singing regardless of the context. In China, Auntie Ping was a riverboat gambler whose real passion was singing. However, she could not find any singing work. She migrated to Australia in search of a better life, and now she is an officer in the Danish Imperial Navy who lives in a beautiful mansion in France. At any rate, I soon realize that I do not have time to think any further about Auntie Ping or singing or anything else. This is because the bells of the abbey have started ringing. I am going to be late for chapel so I run to the abbey. At the abbey, Sister Berthe smugly informs me that I have been summoned to see Mother Superior. I go to Mother Superior's office and I wait nervously outside until, eventually, it is time for me to enter. Inside her office, Mother Superior is waiting at her desk for me. She asks me to come to her. I immediately rush over and kiss her hand and apologize for being late for chapel.

I tell her that I just couldn't help myself and that I had to go to the hills to think. I confess that, lately, I cannot seem to stop thinking about anything and everything—I want to query and ponder every angle and possibility of so many issues. Mother Superior nods and declares that I certainly seem to engage in a lot of reflection and questioning. She then takes my hands and gently tells me that perhaps my vocational strengths are better suited to another industry. She pauses before informing me that she would like to make arrangements for me to look after the children of a Captain von Trapp. I immediately kiss Mother Superior's hand again and I beg her to let me finish my training as a nun. However, Mother Superior firmly tells me that it is time for me to leave the abbey for a while.

So, a few days later, I pack my bags and go to Captain von Trapp's impressive-looking villa. Unfortunately, when I meet Captain von Trapp, I find that I do not get along well with him at all. It turns out that he is very cold to me, and I soon become worried about whether he likes me or not. However, via a process of disobeying the Captain's orders, talking with the Captain about '80s television shows and pop songs, and winning the hearts of the von Trapp children and teaching them how to sing the major diatonic scale, Captain von Trapp and I eventually end up becoming much closer. In fact, soon Captain von Trapp and I are having sex and falling in love.

Once we have gotten together, I find myself incredibly drawn to Captain von Trapp, and he to me. We start spending a great deal of time with each other in his villa; we want to be together all the time. As a result, by the end of the month, we are already finishing each other's sentences and laughing at exactly the same time and in exactly the same way. We start dressing alike. We start walking alike. We even start having the same desires and ambitions. At times, I find myself wondering if so much clinginess and commonality between two people is a good thing. How do you solve a problem like co-dependency?

But, the thing is, it eventually becomes apparent that Captain von Trapp and I are not merging in a typical "couples" sense. In fact, it soon becomes obvious that something quite different is happening. What is happening is this: I am becoming more and more like Captain von Trapp. I have begun wearing clothes that are very similar to the Captain's clothes. I have begun to copy the Captain's gestures. I have begun to insist that people call me "Captain." There is so much about the Captain that I like. There is the air of confidence that surrounds him. There is his ability to look so good in a suit. There is the way that his stern manner commands authority. He is wealthy and sophisticated. He is even a good dancer. No wonder I find it incredibly satisfying to become a man who is like Captain von Trapp.

However, this state of affairs soon raises various issues. In particular, the question "How do you solve a problem like co-dependency?" is soon replaced by a more pressing question: "Can who you like to 'do' also be bound up in issues of who you are or want to be?" Unfortunately, Captain von Trapp is in no mood to query and ponder every angle and possibility of this issue. He becomes uneasy about the changes in me and we start to argue about the new me. He tries to take a disciplinary approach. He orders me to stop answering the telephone as him. He becomes angry when other people mistake me for him. He tries to stop me from repeating everything he says a second after he says it.

I do not blame him for his anger and discomfort but it eventually forces me to flee—not to the hills to think, but straight to the abbey to seek the counsel of the person who first led me to Captain von Trapp.

Inside her office, Mother Superior is waiting at her desk for me. She asks me to come to her. I immediately rush over and kiss her hand, and then I ask her: "Can who you like to 'do' also be bound up in issues of who you are or want to be?" As soon as I voice this question, I fear that Mother Superior will think that I am once again reflecting and questioning too much. Interestingly, Mother Superior does no such thing. Instead, upon hearing my question, she abruptly confesses to me that she has always wanted to have sex with the Fonz from *Happy Days*. As soon as she says this, she looks away from me. But I immediately tell her that I am a huge fan of the Fonz and that I grew up being inspired by the Fonz as a role model of masculinity. When Mother Superior hears this, she looks a little more at ease. I then confess to her my own secret Fonz-related fantasy: I am the Fonz, looking really cool and handsome, and I am standing in the centre of a room wearing a leather jacket and jeans. I snap my fingers. Suddenly, some other really cool and handsome guys wearing leather jackets and jeans run up to me and drape themselves seductively over me and begin stroking my hair. These really cool and handsome guys then snap their fingers. Suddenly, more really cool and handsome guys wearing leather jackets and jeans run up and drape themselves seductively over the first set of really cool and handsome guys and begin stroking their hair. This second set of really cool and handsome guys then snap their fingers. Suddenly, even more really cool and handsome guys wearing leather jackets and jeans run up and drape themselves seductively over this second set of really cool and handsome guys and begin stroking their hair. This pattern continues until the room is completely filled with really cool and handsome guys wearing leather jackets and jeans who are draped seductively over each other and are stroking each other's hair and I as the Fonz am in the centre of it all. Once she hears the relatively more excessive nature of my Fonz-related fantasy, Mother Superior looks relieved. We look at each other and we smile.

Mother Superior then takes my hands and gently tells me that I must find out for myself if who I like to "do" is also bound up in issues of who I am or want to be. She suggests that I escape from Austria and go to Switzerland to try living as someone more like Captain von Trapp. She also adds that if I am impressionable enough to want to become more like someone else, then I should have the courage to live out my fantasy. I kiss Mother Superior's hand again and thank her for her advice. However, I also explain to her that it is simplistic just to say that I am impressionable: in a sense, aren't we all composites of the influences of various entities in our lives—family members, friends, lovers, certain people we watch on TV, characters we read in books, etc., etc.? And surely some of these things are influential because they do appeal to our fantasies? And yet, while our fantasies allow us the pleasure of imagining who we might be, can't they also make us painfully conscious of who we currently are? But Mother Superior is too busy singing the song "Climb Ev'ry Mountain" to listen to me properly. At any rate, Mother Superior is right about me going to Switzerland. So I go and pack for my trip, and then I say my goodbyes to all of the nuns, some of whom seem secretly glad to see me go. The Nazis have closed the borders so I must make the last leg of my journey to Switzerland on foot. But, eventually, I make it to the Austrian Alps and this is where I am to be seen, climbing the mountains to a different kind of life in Switzerland. There I am, walking up a mountain, looking and acting a lot like Captain von Trapp, and thinking about every issue and angle and possibility of my new life while a chorus sings "Climb Ev'ry Mountain," and then there is a wider shot of the surrounding countryside with its lakes and greenery, and then an aerial shot of the mountains and, finally, all you can see are clouds.

LEARNING ENGLISH

When I first arrived in Australia, I did not know
a word of English. I began English lessons through a migrant
settlement program soon after I arrived, but I found it all very
difficult. Yet things did improve a little once I learned the trick
of replacing words I did not know with phrases like "blah blah
blah," "yada yada yada," "whatever," or the name of a celebrity. Australia is very different from my homeland. I was born
and raised in a town called Rod Stewart. Back in those days,
Rod Stewart was a very busy town. The major industries were
David Hasselhoff and coal. I think it is hard for a non-migrant
to understand just how difficult it is to learn a new language
while adapting to life in a new country. Every single day presented me with new frustrations. At the most fundamental
level, I hated not having the necessary words to express myself
and my needs. This was why I hired the actor Bruce Willis to
talk for me. I was inspired by his work as the voice of the baby
in the films *Look Who's Talking* and *Look Who's Talking Too* and
so I decided that Bruce Willis should do my voice. Bruce Willis
flew to Australia to take on the job. He was very blah blah blah.
He ordered for me at restaurants, answered the telephone for
me, spoke to salespeople for me, made prank telephone calls on
my behalf, and more. Like the character of baby Mikey in the
Look Who's Talking films, Bruce Willis gave me an adorable,
wise-cracking personality. Thus, it actually became very useful

for me to have Bruce Willis's voice and I soon became quite popular. But, in the end, I wanted to speak English for myself and so I worked hard to better my command of English and I eventually became independent of Bruce Willis. Like numerous migrants, I picked up a lot of English by watching television. I especially liked watching television shows that featured lawyers, and I used to pay particular attention to plea-bargaining scenes. As a result, my day-to-day speech was soon filled with sentences like, "Murder in the second, twenty to thirty-five years, and we'll drop the conspiracy charge." Some people were impressed by my apparent knowledge of the US legal system. Me, I just felt happy that my English had improved. In fact, last year, I even decided to commemorate the twentieth anniversary of my arrival in Australia by adopting an anglicized name. I turned once again to television for inspiration and began watching repeats of *Fantasy Island* and this is why I now answer to the name "Ricardo Montalbán." However, this morning, my friend Chuck told me that "Ricardo Montalbán" is not quite the right name for me. He said that this is because I am more like "a Chinese version of Heather Locklear." Chuck told me that I am like Heather Locklear in every respect— looks, lifestyle, love life, family, worldview, etc.—except that I am Chinese. Part of me really wanted to believe that Chuck was right but, the thing is, only earlier that day someone else had told me that I am "the Korean equivalent of Oprah Winfrey." I guess I wanted to believe the Oprah thing more. It also occurred to me that, these days, I am definitely doing a lot better in terms of expressing myself and my needs. So I just looked at Chuck and said: "Yada yada yada. Whatever."

TODAY ON DR. PHIL

▼

Today my Auntie Lien and I are appearing on the
television show of the famed psychologist Dr. Phil. The *Dr. Phil*
episode we are appearing in is titled "What are you really mad
at?" and Dr. Phil is asking Auntie Lien and me about how we
deal with anger. Auntie Lien is right in the middle of talking
about her propensity to explode in anger when Dr. Phil asks
her why she gets angry so easily. Auntie Lien hesitates. Dr.
Phil advises her, "You've got to face it to replace it." Hearing
Dr. Phil say this prompts Auntie Lien to confess that her anger
stems from the many difficulties she has experienced with
relationships. She says that she has been unlucky in love.
Furthermore, she says that the sadder she gets, the angrier
she gets. I feel that I can relate to this latter statement and so
I join the studio audience in enthusiastically applauding my
auntie's comment. Auntie Lien suddenly says something in
Ancient Greek. Dr. Phil looks at her blankly, and she explains
that she was quoting from *Medea*, the classic play by Euripides.
She confesses that she likes to study the work of the great
Athenian dramatists. She translates the lines for Dr. Phil:
"The fiercest anger of all, the most incurable / Is that which
rages in the place of dearest love." As Auntie Lien goes on to
discuss in minute detail the structural imperfections in
Euripidean drama that have puzzled scholars for centuries, I
can tell that Dr. Phil and the studio audience are struck by the

fact that they are sharing a room with one of the finest scholars of Ancient Greek drama that the world has seen. Me, I have always found it interesting that Auntie Lien has such a great mind for scholarly pursuits as well as such a great capacity for flying into fits of anger. This makes me think about my own experiences with intellectualism and anger. Sometimes I have a tendency to "intellectualize first and get angry later." Interestingly, like many people, when I get really angry I can transform into what seems like a completely different person. This makes me turn to Dr. Phil to ask him: if anger can transform me, in what other ways might anger be transformative? I suggest to him that perhaps I could use my anger creatively, even proactively. For example, surely some of the most significant political revolutions in history have been in part driven by a sense of rage? This then leads me to consider my attraction to anger. Could it be that I associate anger with power? This would be ironic, given that anger can occur as a consequence of not feeling powerful enough. But Dr. Phil is too absorbed in Auntie Lien's discussion of the function of the chorus in Ancient Greek drama to listen to me properly. However, eventually the topic turns back to anger when Dr. Phil begins reflecting upon the murderous actions of the character of Medea following her betrayal by her husband. In fact, Dr. Phil declares that Medea ably demonstrates his belief that people who experience uncontrollable rage actually have unfulfilled needs that must be addressed. Hearing this makes me think of my own life, and so I confess to Dr. Phil a fantasy that I have recently had. In this fantasy, I become extremely angry. The fantasy begins with me starting to sweat from my anger. My heart starts beating faster.

I clench my fists and the anger makes my face heat up. In this fantasy, I am like the Incredible Hulk in that the angrier I get, the stronger I get. So my muscles start to grow. My muscles become so big that they start to outgrow my clothes. The seams of my shirt and pants begin to split. My neck becomes thicker, and my thighs and calves swell and become harder. I am growing and growing, putting on height as well as bulk, and soon I am around eight feet tall and full of strength and fury. First I go rampaging through the streets, smashing things out of sheer anger. No one is stronger than me. I can bend lamp posts and break walls and throw cars. It does not take long for the police and the military to be sent after me. But they cannot stop me. Their guns and explosives only make me angrier and stronger. I rip apart their trucks and tanks. Then I move on to the sheer satisfaction of destroying whole buildings. After a good hour of smashing and destroying, I stomp all the way to the house of my girlfriend, Tara. Tara opens the door and looks a little surprised to see me. I am standing before her, breathing hard and still very angry. She says to me, "I was just watching you on the news. You were destroying all these buildings. You should have more respect for the property of others." I pause for a moment before replying, "Don't make me angry. You wouldn't like me when I'm angry." I enjoy saying this line to her—it is what Dr Banner used to say before he turned into the Hulk. But, as it turns out, Tara does like me when I'm angry. She begins looking at my muscles in admiration. I glare at her but that only makes her sigh happily. This just makes me glare at her all the more. I am so angry. The angrier I get, the stronger I get. And the stronger I get, the more aroused she gets. She looks at me and her face begins to flush. Her breath starts to quicken. And the more aroused she gets, the younger she gets. She used to be thirty-three but now she is getting younger. She smiles and winks at me as she goes back into her twenties. Fascinated, I watch as she gets younger and younger, and she doesn't stop until she is in her teens and blushing and cuter than ever. And the younger she gets, the fewer people she has had sex with. She slips her hand into mine and tells me that she is sixteen years old and a virgin and that she is eager for me to teach her all about sex. So I scoop her up in my arms and take her to her bedroom and we spend all night having the hottest sex you can imagine. After I have finished telling Dr. Phil my anger fantasy, there is complete silence in the studio. I had been hoping that the audience would enthusiastically applaud my fantasy but they just stare at me. It is then that I wonder if I have said too much. Finally, Dr. Phil breaks the silence to tell me, "You have to name it before you can claim it," and he encourages me to look inside myself to work out what I really want in life. He then says that unfortunately we have run out of time and so he faces the camera to deliver a final address about the issues we have spoken about today. He begins to deliver a very moving address about how life is managed, not cured. As Dr. Phil speaks, I think about the pain that anger can cause and I start to feel sad. I look at Auntie Lien's face and I can tell that she is feeling sad about this too. In fact, the more poignantly Dr. Phil speaks, the sadder Auntie Lien gets. But then I remember that the sadder Auntie Lien gets, the angrier she gets. I soon notice that she is clenching and unclenching her fists. Her eyes dart around the room in agitation. As Dr. Phil continues to speak, she begins to mutter under her breath. Finally, it is too much for her. She explodes in anger, jumping out of her seat and attacking Dr. Phil. Security guards run up to the stage and try to pull Dr. Phil and Auntie Lien apart. The studio audience is hollering and chanting and Auntie Lien is swearing so colourfully that her words will have to be bleeped out before the episode goes to air. Auntie Lien calls out to encourage me to join in the fisticuffs. I am unsure about this but she reminds me that releasing anger can be very satisfying. The thing is, Auntie Lien has a point—quite a valid point that not even Dr. Phil has raised. But first, I take the time to intellectualize about Dollard et al.'s "Frustration-Aggression Hypothesis" and its subsequent behaviourist/neo-associationist reformulation by Berkowitz. Having considered this and its implications for research on factors affecting aggression, I become angry and join Auntie Lien in releasing my rage. As Auntie Lien and I engage in a dramatic punch-up with Dr. Phil and his security guards, the show's end credits start to roll. A few people in the studio audience begin to applaud. Auntie Lien and I still have plenty of rage left but, soon, the show will be over.

CHINESE WHISPERS

1. Chinese Whispers

I know a game called *Chinese Whispers*.

How to play Chinese Whispers:

One person whispers something to the person next to them. The receiver then whispers what the first person said to a third person. This third person whispers the message to a fourth person, and the message is passed on in this way until all the players have heard the message.

The object is to see how much the message will change along the way.

I know a game called *Chinese Whispers*.

How to play Chinese Whispers:

One person whispers something to a receiver. The message is passed on until all the players have heard the message in Chinese.

The object is to change the message to Chinese.

I know a game called *Chinese Whispers*.

How to play Chinese Whispers:

One person whispers something to a receiver. The message is passed on until all the players have become Chinese.

The object is to see how much the people will change along the way.

2. Chinese Burn

A *Chinese burn* is a form of playground punishment or torture. It is also called an *icicle* or a *Japanese burn*, but I know it as a Chinese burn. To inflict a Chinese burn, you rotate the victim's skin near the wrist in opposing directions. This causes friction burns or a sensation of heat in the victim's forearm.

In recognition of the enduring popularity of the Chinese burn, Sega has recently released the game *Virtua Chinese Burn*. This game is currently available on all major gaming consoles.

A *Chinese burn* is a form of torture. It is also known as a *Japanese icicle* or *forearm friction*. To inflict a Chinese burn, a victim is required. The victim and the torturer should be from opposing directions.

Sega has recently released the game *Virtua Chinese Burn*. This game is currently popular.

Those who have popularity in the playground inflict *Chinese burns* on others as a form of torture. This causes a sensation. This causes friction.

Sega recently released *Virtua Chinese Burn*.

At home, the victims play this game on their gaming consoles. They inflict Chinese burns on other, virtual victims to reach a high score.

In the playground, they still receive real Chinese burns.

I know a game called *Chinese burn*. How to play Chinese burn:

A *Chinese burn* is a form of punishment or torture. It is inflicted by the popular.

To be popular is to have recognition.

Popularity is a game.

The victims recognise that popularity is dependent only upon the friction between those who are popular and those who are not popular. The torturers inflict their *Chinese burns* and become popular. A Chinese burn causes a sensation of heat until the forearm is released.

Popularity is a game. Those who are not popular learn to play along.

3. Elvis Presley

Elvis Presley was born to white parents. In this respect, one would say that Elvis was not Asian. However, Asians claimed Elvis from the moment he began incorporating martial arts movements into his performances. When Elvis' *Aloha from Hawaii* television special was broadcast in various Asian countries, it was highly popular. It caused a sensation.

Today, there are Elvis fan clubs all over Asia. There are Asian Elvis impersonators across the world. In addition, karaoke and Elvis are made for each other.

Thangyouveramuch.

Elvis Presley was born in Hawaii. Elvis and Asians are made for each other. Elvis performed martial arts in various Asian countries. It was highly popular. It was special.

Today, Elvis is veramuch broadcast in karaoke all across the world.

Elvis had respect for his parents. Elvis performed martial arts. Elvis performed karaoke.

I know that the white Elvis is an impersonator. Elvis Presley was born veramuch Asian.

Thangyou.

4. Nagasaki

There is a song called "Nagasaki."

"Nagasaki" was written in 1928 by two Americans. The lyrics to part of the first verse are:

> *Hot ginger and dynamite*
> *There's nothing but that at night*
> *Back in Nagasaki*
> *Where the fellers chew tobaccy*
> *And the women wicky wacky woo*

There is a city called Nagasaki.

On August 9, 1945, America bombed the city of Nagasaki. Two Americans were in the plane that dropped the bomb. The bomb was filled with ginger, tobaccy, and plutonium. It was equivalent to twenty-two kilotons of hot dynamite. They bombed the wicky wacky woo out of the city. At least 73,000 fellers, women, and children died. They were given real burns.

A *Chinese burn* causes a sensation of heat.

The message is passed on until all the players have changed along the way.

A COUNTING RHYME

One, two, buckle my shoe. Two, one, steamed pork bun.

Reg Grundies. Undies. Steamed pork buns in your Reg Grundies.

Gregory Peck. Neck. Ginger Meggs. Legs.

Big toe. Tom Cho. Knee. Jenny Kee.

Two, three. Chinese tea.

Tits. Show us your bacon bits.

You look nice. Special combination fried rice.

Nice tits. You've got a special combination of bacon bits.

Phwoar! Four. Open the door.

Five, six. Pick up chicks.

Arse. Shitter. Banana fritter.

Six, seven. Soon-Yi Previn.

Eight. Mate. China plate.

Kitchen sink. Chink.

Ginger beer. Queer.

A Chinese queer. A kitchen sink of ginger beer.

THE BODYGUARD

Someone is stalking Whitney Houston and I have been hired to be her bodyguard. However, I soon discover that guarding Whitney Houston is not as easy a job as I might have thought. It turns out that she and I do not get along very well. She complains that my protection of her is too strict and that she cannot do what she wants to anymore. As a result, even as she becomes more and more frightened of the stalker, she begins acting up. I do not take very well to her acting up so I start acting more aloof. This behaviour soon becomes a pattern for us. Interestingly, even in times when strong emotions are present, I have a tendency—perhaps mechanistically—to call on my sense of logic. Thus, I express to Whitney Houston the following either/or statement: either she will continue to refuse my protection and end up being gruesomely killed by the stalker whom I will eventually track down and apprehend and then and only then will I write a bittersweet yet poignant song about my love for her such that her sister will become very jealous of my talent, or she will allow me to protect her and this will create a better dynamic between us and we will fall in love and one night we will end up having sex at my place and then and only then will I modify my body such that I will be able to defeat her stalker. Presented with these options, Whitney Houston decides that the latter scenario is best. Thus, we end up sleeping together the following night.

Later that night, as we lie together on my bed, I hold her and she rests her head upon my chest and tells me that she has never felt this safe before. This makes me feel proud. Although I have never been the strongest or even the most fearless of my peers, I have always had romantic ideas about being the protector of all the girls. On the other hand, I cannot help feeling that, by sleeping with my client, I have breached the limits of acceptable bodyguard–client relations. So, the next morning, I tell Whitney Houston that we should not have slept together and that we must revert to a proper bodyguard–client relationship. Whitney Houston is very upset about this and we begin to argue and Whitney Houston soon begins acting up and so I start acting more aloof. Eventually, Whitney Houston falls silent for a moment and then she tells me that she is in love with me and that she wants to be with me. I do not know how to respond to this, so I say nothing.

Over the next few weeks, the tension between Whitney Houston and me worsens. She is hurt and angry, and she becomes increasingly uncooperative about receiving my protection. One night, she holds a party at a hotel after one of her performances. At the party, I stand in a corner drinking a vanilla protein shake as I watch her mingling with her guests. She looks truly beautiful, as always. It is then that I notice that Greg Portman is at the party. Portman is a bodyguard I have worked with before. I walk over to Portman and greet him. He says hello in return, and he tells me that he is guarding another one of the guests at the party. We begin chatting. As always, Portman starts talking about some of the recent technological innovations that have been changing the face of bodyguarding.

He tells me that, thanks to major advances in the development of force fields, bionic limbs and cybernetic exoskeletons, his job as a bodyguard has become so much easier. I give Portman's brawny bionic arms a sideways glance before launching into my usual response that I am not interested in adopting any of these technological advances into my bodyguarding work. Portman looks at my biceps and then he laughs at me and tells me that I am still the same old-fashioned guy with my bodyguard fantasies of being chivalrous and protecting women. Sometimes I regret having told Portman about my fantasies of chivalry. Just as Portman begins telling me that going bionic is the best thing that ever happened to him, Whitney Houston comes up to us. I smile at her but she ignores me and smiles at Portman instead. She places her hand on his arm and asks him to tell her all about bionics. As Portman begins to tell her about his very first experience with a neurostimulation implant, I walk away from them and head out to the balcony. On the balcony, I look out at the cityscape. As always, I find myself wishing that I was a stronger and tougher man—a man who is indestructible. After a while, I come to a decision: it is time for me to seek expert advice about my situation.

So, a few days later, I meet up with someone who has a special place in my life. I have always thought of him as a strong and tough man. He is also someone who has had many sexual adventures with women over the years. This person is my Uncle Shen. Uncle Shen has always projected a very physical and confident kind of masculinity. It is a type of masculinity that attracts many women to him and, as a result, I suspect that he is an expert on matters relating to women and desire.

Over beers at a pub, I tell Uncle Shen about what has been happening between Whitney Houston and me. I then mention to him that I have always admired his masculinity and the way it attracts women. Upon hearing this, Uncle Shen confesses that he has modelled aspects of his masculinity on Marlon Brando's animalistic, swaggering portrayal of Stanley Kowalski in the film *A Streetcar Named Desire*. He says that he saw the film as a teenager and was struck by the sexual power of Brando's Kowalski. He adds that he loves the power of having women want him, and he begins talking about his experiences of having flings with girls he meets in bars. Smiling, he tells me that his favourite line from *A Streetcar Named Desire* is, "I have always depended on the vaginas of strangers." He says that he has adopted this line as his life philosophy. I do not have the heart to tell Uncle Shen that he has based his life philosophy on misquoting Tennessee Williams, so I simply nod and tell him that I understand. Uncle Shen then winks and tells me that he has had many pleasurable journeys on "the streetcar named desire." Me, I can only think about how some of my deepest desires are unattainable, so I say nothing. Uncle Shen notices that I have gone quiet. He tells me that there are too many good things about desire for one to get too sad about it. He adds that the opposite situation—a life without desire—would be far worse. In spite of my mood, I can't help seeing some truth in what he is saying. So, as Uncle Shen begins talking about some of the things he finds attractive in women, I smile and join in, and we spend the rest of the evening discussing our interest in "a streetcar named lingerie."

After saying goodbye to Uncle Shen, I head back to Whitney

Houston's mansion. She is waiting up for me and wants to talk. She apologizes for her behaviour toward me. As I look at her in surprise, she confesses that she is very scared of the stalker and that she wants my protection now more than ever. She also mentions that she has been nominated for an Oscar and that, even though it may be dangerous, she wants to go to the awards ceremony. I congratulate her on her nomination. She blushes and thanks me. I look at her and I realize that, tonight, among my many desires, I want to continue protecting her and being her bodyguard. I tell her that she can go to the awards ceremony and that I will look after her. She smiles and thanks me again. As she walks away in her baby pink satin slip with its lace detail, side split, and embroidered contrast trim, I also make a silent vow to myself that I will do whatever is necessary to ensure that she is safe.

On Oscars night, Whitney Houston is understandably nervous about her safety. Cameras and lights and crowds of fans and actors and technicians are everywhere, and she looks almost ill with worry. I look at her with concern and I realize that it was a mistake for me to have told her my theory that the stalker was going to strike tonight. Fortunately, the night gets much better for her when, four and a half hours later, it is announced that she has won her award. When the announcement is made, she raises her hands to her face in shock. The orchestra begins playing and everyone applauds as she makes her way to the stage. As she walks up to the podium to accept her award, I turn around and am surprised to see Portman standing near me. I greet him but he looks a little awkward as he says hello in return. It is then that I realize the truth:

Portman is the stalker and he is at the Oscars to launch his ultimate attack on Whitney Houston. Sure enough, just as Whitney Houston is about to make her acceptance speech, I notice that Portman's left bionic eye has begun to glow red. I immediately run out onto the stage and make a flying leap in front of Whitney Houston and push her out of the way. A laser beam from Portman's eye hits me in the shoulder. Everyone in the auditorium screams. I stand up and face Portman, my shoulder wound closing in a matter of seconds. He is shocked to see my wound heal so quickly. I inform him that I have changed since we last met at the party and that, while I am still not the strongest or even the most fearless of my peers, I too have embraced some of the more recent technological innovations that have been changing the face of bodyguarding. I explain that I have always wanted to be indestructible and I have now acquired super-fast healing powers and had my entire skeleton laced with an alloy that is designed to withstand extreme pressures. Portman suddenly activates his personal force field and tells me that, as long as I can never land a hit on him, he will be undefeatable. In response, I flex my bionic hands into fists and I unsheathe three foot-long super-sharp metal claws from each fist. Everyone in the auditorium screams again as Portman and I begin to fight. However, it is not long before I have Portman on the defensive. Once he realizes how powerful I have become, his confidence begins to fade. Eventually, I am able to corner him and slash through his force field with my claws. Yet, just as I deliver the final blow to defeat Portman, he fires one last blast from his bionic eye into my chest. This blast is delivered from virtually point-blank range. As Portman sinks to the ground, I fall backwards, blood pouring from my chest. Whitney Houston screams and rushes over to cradle me in her arms. She cries and begs me not to die on her. Crowds of people are surrounding us as Whitney Houston holds my body. My blood spills onto her clothes and she pleads with me to hold on and stay with her. But, once again, my wound heals in a matter of seconds, and Whitney Houston and I look at each other and we smile.

A week later, Whitney Houston and I are saying our farewells on an airport tarmac. She is doing her best to not cry. We talk briefly but soon it is time for us to part so I kiss her on the cheek and we hug each other and tell each other goodbye. She walks away from me and enters her private plane. The plane's engine starts and she sits and looks at me from her seat at the window. As I watch the plane slowly turn away and begin taxiing down the runway, I find myself feeling very sad. It seems that I am not indestructible after all. However, I also suddenly realize that there is something else that I desire more than pure indestructibility. Thus, I formulate the following either/ or statement: either I will stoically watch the plane depart and Whitney Houston will get the pilot to stop the plane so that she can run out to kiss me and then and only then will I resume my life as a bodyguard without her such that she will end up singing a song about our relationship, or I will decide that there is no logical reason why I cannot be her bodyguard as well as her lover so I will make a flying leap onto one of the plane's wings and unsheathe my claws and use them to rip a hole in the side of the plane so that I can climb in and grab Whitney Houston and we can kiss and then and only then will I tell her that I have come to realize that being a bodyguard who can also be her lover—and being a bionic man who can also be human—is ultimately what I desire such that she will let herself be held by me and she will offer me an ongoing contract to work as both her bodyguard and her lover. Presented with these options, I decide that the latter scenario is best. Thus, Whitney Houston ends up in my arms, smiling at me, and offering to discuss the terms of my contract.

AIYO!!! AN EVIL GROUP OF NINJAS IS ENTERING AND DESTROYING A CALL CENTRE!!!

AIYO!!! An evil group of ninjas is entering and destroying a call centre!!!

Blood everywhere!!! Die-lah! So much weapons, killing here, killing there! The call centre operators are getting cut up by ninja swords, left, right and centre! The ninjas are throwing so many throwing stars into the team leaders' eyes-lah ... they must be professional killers-man!

Aiyo! Hear the dying fellas screaming! Call centre targets, sure cannot reach-one today!

The ninjas now got big tanks and big weapons to destroy everything! Alamak! Look out, young lady—get away from your work station! Aiyah, a missile langgar her!!! Wasted! She so pretty-lah!

Ay! What's happening to the young lady?! She still not yet dead! Her body connecting back together!!! Her brains that are on the floor now flow back into her head! Her internal organs repairing themselves also! Hemorrhaging also finish! Wah! Now her face is cute again!

Aiyo! What about her legs-lah?! She got no legs! During the explosion her legs got blown off far, far away! Aiya! She needs legs-lah!!!

Wah! She damn good with computers, ah! She dismantle a PC from her colleague work desk and use the parts to make new legs for herself! Wah! Now she become a deadly cyborg!!!

She got killer laser beam eyes! She got a flamethrower mouth! She got red boots like Astro Boy! Wah-liao! She is the most powerful killer machine ever invented-man!!!

Wah! Now she go and make friends with the office equipment! She is talking to the network server, the fax, the photocopier, the laser printer, the palm pilots and the calculators in so many different computer languages!

Now she modify the office equipment! Now the network server can walk and even fire atomic ray! And even the fax can fly and drop smart bomb! Wah-liao! Now she got a super-destructo-killer army—terror-man this girl! Cutting edge of office technology-lah!!!

Look! She and her army are fighting with the group of evil ninjas! Wah! Massacre-lah—ninja blood and bodies everywhere!!! Shock-lah! Now no more ninjas left because they all die already!

Wah-liao! This ex-call centre operator terror-lah! She win the war with the ninjas! She is the best cyborg killer in the universe!

Aiyah! She even eating the remains of all the ninja warriors! Wah, and now she is offering to buy cappuccino for everybody!!! So polite-ah-she!

I, ROBOT

⋮

▼

The year is 2136 and the Australian government has
recently launched a new program for low-income earners. This
program is perhaps a little radical: people who sign up for the
program are converted into robots and given new employment
opportunities. Many people are wary of this program and it has
not been very popular so far. Me, I am intrigued by the program
and I have decided to sign up for it. Some might say that I
am interested in doing this because my mother was one of the
program's first success stories. She completed it two years ago,
when it was run as a pilot project. Now she has a total linear
computational speed of over six trillion operations per second.
She has also moved from her human job in Melbourne—as an
assembler of car parts in a manufacturing plant for the Ford
Motor Company—to a robot job in New York—as an assembler of car parts in a manufacturing plant for the Ford Motor
Company. She is even capable of transforming from her robot-
self into a gold 1977 Holden Sunbird hatchback and from this
Holden Sunbird back to her robot-self again.

My mother and I do not always get along but, given her high
opinion of the program, I am confident that she will be glad
that I want to sign up. Sure enough, when I telephone her one
night to break this news to her, she says that she is pleased
about my decision. I take a risk and confide in her: I tell her
that I have always had perfectionist tendencies and thus the

precision and unerring competence of robots is very appealing to me. There is a pause as my mother thinks this over, but she soon declares that this is a fair enough reason for joining the program. I am relieved that she understands this. Then she adds that I sometimes have a problem with respecting authority and so maybe becoming a robot could help me with this too. Although I am not as enthused about hearing this latter piece of feedback, I tell my mother that I will keep her comment in mind.

The very next day, I apply to join the program. The application process turns out to be quite bureaucratic. I am required to read a large amount of documentation about job skilling opportunities for robots, attend long meetings with caseworkers and fill in many forms to verify my identity. Finally, after a few months, my entry application is approved. On my first day as a new recruit, the program's scientists welcome me to the program. They then take me to a testing room so they can administer a wide range of psychological tests to assess what type of robot I should be. As well as completing many questionnaires, these tests involve me doing puzzles of different types while being observed by the scientists. In the end, it takes me a whole day to complete all of the tests. A few days later, I meet with the scientists again to receive my test results. According to the scientists, my results indicate that I am best suited to being a protocol droid. The scientists inform me that, as a protocol droid, I will be programmed in etiquette and language use, and I will assist politicians, diplomats and other officials to ensure that important interactions run smoothly. I am unsure about my suitability as a protocol droid and I warn the scientists that I am not very good at following protocols. I add that I was recently told that I sometimes have a problem with respecting authority. While the scientists admit that my results for the Myers-Briggs Type Indicator personality test are troubling, they tell me that I seem to have an aptitude for language use and thus they are convinced that I would function well as a protocol droid. I am just about to pull out of the whole deal when the scientists tell me that, as a protocol droid, I will receive specialist programming in understanding human behaviour. They also declare that I will be fluent in over six million forms of communication, I will be able to decipher codes and I will have the ability to write brilliantly in any style and genre. Upon hearing this, I decide that I want to go ahead with everything.

Over the next few months, the scientists transform me into a protocol droid. This transformation turns out to be quite a significant process. By the end, while I am humanoid in basic appearance, every aspect of my body has changed. I have golden plating for skin. I have a hyperalloy endoskeleton for bones. Where my eyes should be, there are spectral-analyzers. As promised by the scientists, I am also equipped with a special communicator module and a new top-of-the-line positronic brain to give me highly advanced linguistic abilities. I now even speak with a prestigious-sounding British accent. Perhaps more than anything, I had envisioned that becoming a robot would make me completely logic-driven, reliable and without any emotional frailties. However, as it turns out, I am prone to anxiety and vexation, rather like C-3PO from *Star Wars*. Yet, despite this problem, I adhere to the terms of my contract with the government and I begin my new working life as a robot the next day. I am assigned to work in the area of international security. This work requires me to perform interpreting and protocol-related duties for politicians and United Nations representatives. I am also required to travel to some of the world's major cities.

Unfortunately, I soon realize that working in the area of international security is no place for someone who is prone to anxiety. As my work in this area progresses, I begin fretting more and more, just like C-3PO. In fact, after a few weeks, the scientists from the program take me aside to inform me that they have been receiving complaints from some of the politicians and officials I have been assisting. The scientists tell me that my constant interjections of "Secret mission? What plans? What are you talking about?" and "This is madness—we'll be destroyed for sure!" are proving disruptive to meetings. The scientists attempt to reduce my anxiety by converting my main interlink sequencer to asynchronous operation. At first, this seems to work, but my anxiety slowly begins to return. In fact, one afternoon at the United Nations Headquarters in Manhattan, an incident arises at a meeting of the United Nations Security Council where I am working. The Council is right in the middle of discussing issues regarding the use of nuclear, chemical and biological weapons when I interrupt the discussion by pointing at the Security Council President and crying out "He's holding a thermal detonator! We're doomed!" Everyone stares at me. The Council President tersely informs me that he is not holding a thermal detonator and he asks me if I am experiencing a malfunction. I tell him that I had warned the scientists who created me that I am not very good at following protocols. He says that I should nonetheless immediately report to the Information Technology Services Division for repairs. I tell the Council President that I would prefer not to do this and I add that I had also warned the scientists who created me that I sometimes have a problem with respecting authority. Frowning, the Council President calls in two security guards to escort me from the room. The two guards approach me. I tell them to stay away but they keep walking toward me. At this point, something in me changes. Although I am programmed for etiquette rather than violence, my positronic brain begins to initiate processes for engaging in destruction. Furthermore, I begin to transform again. The two security guards and the entire Security Council watch in amazement as I complete my transformation in only a couple of minutes. When I have finished I stand before them, gleaming. I have plasma cannons for arms. I have tactical dreadnought armour for golden plating. Where my spectral-analyzers should be, there are nano-disrupters. The Council President reminds me of the spirit of United Nations Security Council Resolution 1265 regarding armed conflict, but I tell him that I do not care. As my plasma cannons begin to glow, he protests that I am programmed for protocol only. But I simply inform him that I am following in a tradition practiced by many other robots and humans in history: that of seeming to go haywire, and then turning on one's masters and what they stand for. As I begin destroying the Security Council chamber with concentrated plasma blasts, everyone screams and runs from the room. Other groups of security guards soon enter the chamber to subdue me.

But when they see how powerful my plasma cannons are, they drop their blaster rifles and phasers and Varon-T disruptors, and they begin fleeing from me too. As these guards retreat down the corridor in terror, I ignore them so that I can continue firing my plasma cannons at the Security Council chamber. A minute or so later, once the chamber has been completely destroyed, I take a moment to enjoy a sense of satisfaction. Then I turn my attention to the rest of the premises—I make my way through the United Nations Headquarters, destroying various offices, meeting chambers and assembly areas. As I move from room to room firing my plasma cannons, representatives from every nation in the world flee from me. People of all creeds, colours and walks of life are evacuating the building because of my might. When I eventually emerge from the building, I find a line of TX-130T fighter tanks waiting for me. I see the familiar insignia on the tanks and I realize that it has not taken long for the United Nations to assemble a peacekeeping force to restore order. A great battle between me and the peacekeeping force begins. Although I have become extremely powerful, I am aware that a fleet of TX-130Ts poses a major challenge to my might. Sure enough, as the battle goes on and the fighter tanks fire successive laser cannon blasts at me, I end up sustaining a significant amount of damage. Nonetheless, I am able to fight on and defeat most of the troops. In the end, surrounded by burning tanks and property, I am left facing just one surviving fighter tank. I am expecting the tank to fire directly at me but instead it fires at an overhanging section of the building that I am standing under. The heavy structure falls on top of me, almost burying me completely. A soldier climbs out of the tank and surveys the scene. He says, "It's over. Finally, it's over." But it is not over: he is shocked as I rise slowly from the debris. My armour has been completely destroyed, leaving my endoskeleton exposed. I look down at the bareness of my endoskeleton for a moment. Then I register the soldier in my targeting system and my plasma cannons begin to glow again. But suddenly the surviving tank accelerates, mowing down and crushing my body before coming to a halt. The soldier surveys the scene again. He says, "It's over. Finally, it's over." But it is not over: my mangled body completely regenerates and I stand before my enemies and I destroy them all. As I look at the remains of all the fighter tanks and the ruins of the United Nations Headquarters, I take a moment to absorb what has happened. Slowly and a little painfully, I transform myself into the car I always wanted as a child—a blue and white Ford Bronco 4x4—and then I drive myself away from the United Nations Headquarters.

I drive for an hour or so, making my way through the noise and traffic of Midtown Manhattan. I drive down long street blocks, heading further and further away from the skyscrapers and busy crowds, past the tourist landmarks and billboards. I eventually make my way out of the commercial district, finding myself in some of Manhattan's residential neighbourhoods. As the flow of traffic eases and my surroundings become quieter and less cluttered, I feel a little calmer. Finally, as I drive down a pretty, tree-lined street, I pull over to the side of the road. I make one more transformation: I transform myself back into a human. More precisely, I transform back to my former self— although I make myself just a few inches taller and with bigger biceps. I look at my watch and see that it is almost four o'clock in the afternoon. I decide that I will find a place to sleep for the night so that, tomorrow, I can try to make my way back home. However, as I begin walking down the street, a gold 1977 Holden Sunbird hatchback pulls up beside me. I stop and wait as my mother transforms from her car-self into her robot-self. Once she has made her transformation, she and I look at each other. I do not say anything; I wait to hear what she will say to me. After a moment, my mother tells me that she knows about my actions at the United Nations Headquarters. I immediately think that she is going to lecture me for the destruction that I have caused. However, to my surprise, she does not do this. She simply shrugs and tells me, "You always had to do things differently from everyone else." I have heard her say this to me before. However, when I hear it this time, it does not seem like an insult—more a statement of fact. She even looks impressed when I subsequently boast that, in defeating the United Nations peacekeeping force, I defeated an army representing the entire world. She reminds me that she had always raised me to stand up for myself. I nod in agreement. She smiles at me and then she transforms back into a Holden Sunbird. She opens up her front passenger door and she encourages me to get in. She says that she will help me to make my way back home. Feeling tired, I step into the car and relax into the warm vinyl seat. She begins playing a cassette of her favourite classic rock hits and this makes me smile. Then she closes her door, starts up her engine and drives us away.

MY LIFE IN CHINA

▼

Few people in the whole of China could run as fast, jump as high, or catch as many deer that could run as fast or jump as high as my grandmother. The whole village relied on my grandmother for food during the winter season.

My grandmother's best friend was named Gerty. Gerty was once an outstanding hunter herself. In the summer, Gerty liked to wander the plains in search of caribou to shoot. In the winter, she liked to ski the slopes of Shanghai. But a rail accident put an end to both her hunting and skiing days. The driver of the train was named Bo.

Bo's brother, Bob, built trucks for a living. Bob's own car was a hotted-up Pontiac GTO with the fattest tires in all of China. Bob, Carlos and Jimbo would take the car to Beijing on weekends to race in illegal street-racing meets. Jimbo once bought a set of genuine customized, chrome mag wheels from a woman named Velma for a steal—only $4 for the whole set. Velma dealt in mag wheels and the finest skins and pelts.

Velma's cousin Artie played in a jazz trio with his friends Mort and Sid. Sid played double-bass and he got the trio a gig at an outdoor concert in Toisan. The concert was rained out. The promoter of the concert, Al, met Suzie at a bar that night.

Suzie was a gorgeous dame, a real looker. She was a tall, busty, femme bitch top who was seeking non-scene, straight-acting men.

She said to Al, "What's your name?"

Al said, "My name is Suzie."

Suzie said, "It's good to meet you, Suzie."

They went to a motel and they did it all through the night. It was the first time Suzie had ever done it with a man who had the same name as her.

The character of Suzie will now be played by Dick Sargent, who is perhaps best known for playing the role of Darrin on *Bewitched*. Dick is genuinely excited about this latest role. He will call upon all the skills he has developed over the course of his successful career in television. He plans to accentuate Suzie's ambitious side and also to allow some of her trust issues to interplay more with the vulnerabilities of other characters.

A year later, Suzie—the Suzie who was Al, that is—had moved to the south of China and was operating a fishing trawler. The cabin boy on board the trawler, Clarence, always said that fish tasted more like snake than venison. Clarence had originally boarded the trawler as a stowaway from Taiwan.

As it turns out, I see Clarence all the time. These days, he is the closest person I have to a father.

I have never been to the village that was reliant on my grandmother for food during the winter season. However, few people in the whole of China—my grandmother being one of those few—can run as fast, jump as high, or catch as many deer that can run as fast or jump as high as me.

PINOCCHIO

The year is 1981 and I am driving down the streets of Melbourne in my blue and white Ford Bronco 4x4. I am going to Tara's house for a surprise visit. Feeling excited about the prospect of seeing her, I arrive at her house and I ring the doorbell. When Tara answers the door, I smile at the sight of her. She is looking very pretty in a long black skirt and a lacy pink top. I greet her and I reach out to hug her. However, she only looks at me in shock, which quickly turns to anger. She tells me that she has not heard from me in at least a year. She says that she had thought everything had been going really well in our relationship and then, all of a sudden, I had stopped contacting her. It seemed that I had left town without telling anyone. She had tried many ways of contacting me, all unsuccessful, and in the end, she had been torn between being worried about me and being angry. After Tara has finished saying this, she looks at me and I can see the hurt in her eyes. I apologize to her. I tell her that there is a good reason for my absence but that I am afraid to reveal this to her because I fear that she will not believe me. She says that she deserves an explanation. I know that she has just made a good point, so I take a deep breath and I tell her my story.

About fifteen months ago, I became determined to realize a dream I had—to be a guest star on *The Muppet Show*. I had already spent a few years watching *The Muppet Show* and fantasizing that I was the person being surrounded by Muppets and singing with them. Now I wanted to see if I could actually appear on *The Muppet Show*. So I set about contacting the producers of the show and entered into a protracted series of secret negotiations with them. At one stage, it looked as if I would never achieve my ambition. The producers had a long list of reasons why I should not be a guest star on their show, the main one being that I was not famous. But, amazingly, after a few months of discussion that seemed to go nowhere, the producers suddenly informed me that I would be their next guest star. Thus, after the contracts were signed, I ended up flying to Hollywood to make my guest appearance with the Muppets. On the day I was scheduled to do the taping, I was very excited. I showed up to the studio right on time and was taken directly into the Makeup and Wardrobe Department to prepare for my stint in front of the cameras. I do not remember very much about my experience at the Makeup and Wardrobe Department. All I remember is that a team of stylists surrounded me and started arranging my hair and spraying something into my face, and then I suddenly began to feel very sleepy. Later, I woke up in darkness. I was not sure how much time had passed since I had fallen asleep but one thing was for certain: I did not wake up as the same person I was before. Although I was still feeling groggy, I immediately realized that my body was entirely bound up with bandages of some kind. There were even bandages covering my face. I felt almost ill with fear. Then I heard someone come into the room. I listened as this person walked over to me and cheerfully said hello. He introduced himself as Frank, one of the chief makeup artists on

The Muppet Show. He told me to be still and relax, and then he began cutting and unravelling the bandages from my body. He started at my torso. While the bandages were being stripped from my body, I waited fearfully in silence. When the bandages were finally removed from my face, I blinked as my eyes adjusted to the light. Frank—a balding man with a kind-looking face—was smiling at me. He then held a mirror in front of me so that I could see what I looked like. I looked into the mirror and, for a moment, I could not speak. I realized that I had been transformed into a Muppet—more specifically, I was a Muppet penguin—and I knew that this was not a dream. I was outraged and began shouting at Frank in what I realized was quite a squeaky voice. I demanded that he turn me back into my former self. At this point, a man walked into the room. I instantly recognised him. He was Jim Henson, the creator of the Muppets. Jim tried to console me. He told me that being transformed into a Muppet was one step better than being a guest star on *The Muppet Show*. He also told me that the Makeup and Wardrobe team had done a great job on me—he said that I looked really good as a Muppet penguin and he pointed out that I had even been provided with a little orange beanie and a pair of yellow woollen gloves to wear. I started to protest once again and he said that if I met my fellow Muppet cast members, perhaps I would see how good it was to be a Muppet. I shook my head and demanded that I be changed back into a human right away. Jim said that surely I should talk with some of the other Muppets first. He also promised that, if I still wanted to be transformed back into a human by the end of the day, he would arrange for this to happen. This did not sound so bad so I waddled over to him and let him pick me up. Frank smiled and waved goodbye to me, and Jim took me to a studio down the corridor. There were quite a few of the Muppets in this studio. They were lounging around in chairs on one of the empty sets. Most of the well-known Muppets were there, including Kermit the Frog, Miss Piggy, Rowlf, Gonzo, Animal, the Swedish Chef, Fozzie Bear, Statler and Waldorf, Beaker—who is one of my very favourite Muppets—and even Camilla, Gonzo's chicken sweetheart. Jim introduced me to everyone. The other Muppets greeted me and waved and generally seemed very friendly. Jim told me that he would come back and see me a bit later and he left. Although I had not imagined that this would be the way I would end up meeting the Muppets, I began chatting with them. It turned out that all of the Muppets had formerly been humans. For example, the guy who became Kermit the Frog was once a high-profile taxation lawyer from a prestigious law firm who, upon finding himself in a midlife crisis, decided to pursue a career in the arts. One day, he noticed a job advertisement in a newspaper. The advertisement was from a then-unknown company that was seeking an artistic director for a new and innovative multi-art form performance project with culturally and linguistically diverse communities. He answered the advertisement, was hired for the role, and unexpectedly found himself transformed into a Muppet frog named Kermit. He told me that, naturally, he was upset at first but that he now thrives on the thrill of performing, stage managing and leading a struggling arts organization. Another one of the Muppets also had a background in the corporate world. A few years ago, Jim Henson had hired her as a consultant to write a business plan for his rapidly expanding company. As it turned out, Jim and his management staff did not care for her ideas about how to maintain financial viability in balance with artistic integrity. The morning after she had informally suggested a company restructure, she woke up to find herself chained to a drum kit in a basement. She had been transformed into an aggressive Muppet drummer who played the drums with a crazed and violent kind of intensity. Her analytical skills and strategic planning expertise had also disappeared. Instead, these characteristics had been overtaken by raw, primal urges for sex, food, and playing the drums. Yet, after her initial shock at her transformation, she too found a greater sense of fulfilment in her new role. She told me that Jim Henson had done her a favour and that she did not miss her life as a business analyst at all. She said that her new life was so much better now. As I talked with more and more of the Muppets and listened to their testimonials about how much their lives had improved since they had become Muppets and joined *The Muppet Show*, I began to think that perhaps I should give myself the chance to experience a new life as a Muppet. Maybe Jim was right—maybe actually being a Muppet was better than playing a guest role, surrounded by Muppets. So I joined *The Muppet Show* cast and thus began one of the most memorable periods of my life—a period of about a year in which I had opportunity after opportunity to perform with some of the world's most talented actors, dancers and musicians. I was performing with stars such as Harry Belafonte, Liza Minnelli, Danny Kaye, and Rudolf Nureyev, and I was really enjoying these moments. Yet my experiences with *The Muppet Show* were not always filled with such highlights. For example, at one stage, I had to perform song-and-dance numbers with Sylvester Stallone and, months later, Mark Hamill from *Star Wars*. It was around that time that I really began to feel the strain of performing in a weekly vaudeville-style variety show format. I realized that, as much as I had previously loved watching *The Muppet Show*, it was quite a different thing to actually be transformed from a human into a Muppet and then be required to perform on the show. Furthermore, I began to miss the life that I had lived prior to being a Muppet. I had not seen my friends for a long time. I especially missed Tara. After thinking about things for a while, I approached Jim Henson. I told him that, while part of me still enjoyed being a Muppet, I really missed the life that I had left behind. I asked him if I could be transformed back into the person I once was. Jim saw the sad look on my face and he took pity on me. He said that, as long as I stayed until the end of the current season, he would transform me back into my former self and release me from my contract. So, after Episode 24 of Season 5, my work on *The Muppet Show* came to an end. I remember very clearly the last scene I performed in. I was part of a menagerie of Muppets that was accompanying guest star Roger Moore in his closing number. As I listened to Roger singing the final lines of "Talk to the Animals," I knew that leaving the show was the right decision for me.

This is the end of the story that I have to tell Tara and, after I have finished telling it, I wait anxiously for her reaction. She looks at me for a moment. Then she tells me that my story is the most ridiculous thing she has ever heard. She says that it is completely implausible. I start to protest that I am telling the truth but she interrupts me. She asks me how I ever expected her to believe that I became a Muppet penguin who met and performed with a cast of Muppets who were also formerly human. She says that, if I was going to lie to her, I should at least have made my lie feasible. I do not say anything for a moment. Instead, I think about the theory that I had developed about lying. Prior to creating my *Muppet Show* lie, I had conducted research into some of the greatest lies told in the history of humanity and I had come to the conclusion that the greatest lies ever told have the following two major characteristics:

1. The lie is embellished with the appropriate amount of detail.
2. The lie is ultimately about something that, for the time being, the target wants to believe in.

Recalling my elaborate *Muppet Show* lie, I realize that it more or less succeeded on the first point—the lie had enough specific information to make it interesting, yet it was vague enough to carry a hazy sense of authority. However, my *Muppet Show* lie failed on the second point because only I wanted to believe in the fantasy of me being a Muppet. Prior to creating my *Muppet Show* lie, I had spent many moments enjoying the adventures of the Muppets. I loved listening to Fozzie Bear's jokes, I felt envious of Kermit the Frog when Julie Andrews took his hand and sang to him, and I especially enjoyed watching Animal when he wildly played the drums. In contrast, I realize that Tara does not have any investment in the fantasy of me becoming a Muppet. In fact, I am forced to listen as she launches into a negative critique of my Muppet story. She tells me that, while my Muppet story is well-crafted and economically expressed and even provides some compelling insights into the human condition, it suffers from the flaw of being completely unconvincing and thus she was not able to suspend her disbelief. She also accuses me of deliberately inserting the part about missing her just to gain her sympathy. Desperate, I try one last time to convince her that my Muppet story is true and I offer to show her old episodes of *The Muppet Show* where I can be seen as a Muppet penguin. However, she tells me that I am only making things worse by lying more. She reveals that she is a big fan of the Muppets and that she has a growing collection of Muppet memorabilia that includes paintable plastic figurines, keychains, lunchboxes, and even the original 1972 album *The Muppet Musicians of Bremen*. Being such a dedicated Muppet fan, she declares that she knows for a fact that stars like Sylvester Stallone, Liza Minnelli, and Rudolf Nureyev all appeared in different seasons of *The Muppet Show* and that the time that elapsed between these appearances was well over a year. Furthermore, she declares that my nose has started growing. I laugh at this latter statement but she simply points at my face and says that she is telling the truth. I put my hands to my nose and am shocked to realize that she is not lying: my nose is at least five centimetres longer than it originally was. I run to her bathroom to look at myself in the mirror. She follows me and watches as I look at my reflection. I stare sadly at myself. For a few moments, I cannot speak. I just look at myself. After a while, I turn to Tara and I apologize for lying to her. I say that it seems that I have become like Pinocchio—a not-so-real boy who is full of falsehoods and fallibilities. I turn back to the mirror once more. Tara puts her hand on my arm but I do not say anything. Then I feel her hug me. She tells me that Pinocchio was a fascinating and lovable boy precisely because of his frailties and vices. She also declares that, "real boy" or not, Pinocchio was actually at his most interesting when he was a "bad boy." At this point, I become conscious of her leg pressed against mine. I turn to her and she smiles shyly at me. I stare at her for a moment. Then I kiss her roughly and I pull at her hair as I kiss her. We move to her bedroom and I continue to kiss her and I grab handfuls of her here and there and I leave a bite mark on her shoulder and then I strip her clothes off and we spend all night having the hottest sex you can imagine. We do it in a few different ways: first her as a good girl, then her as a bad girl, then her as a good girl who is coerced into being a bad girl. Throughout it all, I am a bad boy who tells good stories. These stories are fantasies. As I tell her these fantasies, I realize that they are aligned with my theory of the greatest lies ever told: each fantasy is embellished with the appropriate amount of detail and it is ultimately about something that, for the time being, the target wants to believe in.

The next morning, I wake up in Tara's bed and I feel good when she moves closer to me and greets me with "Good morning" and kisses me. She playfully touches the tip of my still-long nose. We do not say anything for a moment but then she softly asks me if I have come back for good or if I am going to go away again. I take a moment to consider this. I tell her that, as much as I have so desperately wanted to, I have never been able to predict my own comings and goings. But I also tell her that I would like to stay. Tara smiles and we both start to fantasise about what our future might look like. In embellishing this fantasy with the appropriate amount of detail, we draw inspiration from films we have seen, books we have read, friends we have known, lovers we have had, words we have written, daydreams we have dreamed and much more. As we discuss our fantasy future, we realize that it looks a lot like this: every night, she—a good girl—will turn into a bad girl because she has gotten together with a bad boy, and yet, every day, I—a bad boy—will be redeemed by her love—the love of a good woman—thereby turning me into a good man. We agree that this fantasy is immensely appealing to both of us. Thus, for the time being, the future looks good.

LOOK WHO'S MORPHING

▼

1. Look Who's Morphing

There was a boy who went to sleep as a human but woke up as a dragon. There was a call centre operator who became a deadly cyborg. There was a talking sultana that changed into a box of a very popular brand of cereal, and there was a bottle of beer that turned into a curvaceous woman.

Me, I morphed into a giant reptilian creature. I was exactly like Godzilla, except that I also had a combination of the best qualities of the world's lizards. My skin was thorny and I had long claws on my hands and feat. My tongue was bright blue. As I began my rampage, a giant orange frill of skin flared out dramatically around my neck. I had chosen to attack the leafy eastern suburbs of Melbourne. This was the neighbourhood that I grew up in and now I stomped around its streets, destroying shopping centres, sporting clubs and scout halls while residents screamed in horror. It didn't take long for the government to send the military after me, but I easily destroyed their tanks and fighter jets. My skin then changed colour until it was the same pale blue as the sky above me, and I continued my attack, stepping on libraries, prestigious private schools, and well-kept gardens.

That night, I wandered through the locality, staring at the suburban streets below me. Due to my rampage, these streets were deserted. But I was not wandering aimlessly: I had decided to visit my mother. I took a deep breath and walked to her house. I saw the kitchen light on and I knew that she was home but, as I towered over her house, I felt too afraid to call out to her—I knew she wouldn't be happy to see me like this. I watched her house for a little while but eventually I decided to leave. I was too hungry anyway—I had been wreaking destruction for hours and had not eaten anything. Then I noticed the many neat rows of bok choy and choy sum in my mother's big vegetable garden. As well as being a brilliant gardener, my mother always loved it when I enjoyed her food. Stooping over the house, I tried to be very quiet as I ate her vegetable garden. I ate everything until all that was left was a hole in the ground. However, it didn't taste as good as I thought it would. After I had finished eating my meal, I looked down at what remained of her vegetable garden, and I noticed some blue pellets strewn about. It was then that I remembered how much my mother detested the snails and slugs that ate the plants in her garden—and how she regularly used large doses of snail and slug killer. Half an hour later, I was vomiting all over the municipality of my childhood. Dogs barked in panic. Residents screamed abuse at me as my vomit rained down on their houses. After I had finished, I looked down at the mess I had made and I stomped away in shame. Like Godzilla after a rampage, I was returning to where I lived—not an island, though, but my house on the other side of town. And, like any escaping skink, I was leaving my tail behind.

The next morning, I decided that I needed to change for the better. After some consideration, I morphed into a teen doctor. I became a young man so clever that I got a medical degree when I was fourteen. I began working as a surgeon in a hospital but, despite my brilliance as a surgeon, I still struggled with the many issues that teenagers typically face—body changes brought on by puberty, maintaining friendships with other teenagers, a developing sexual identity, etc. I soon realized that the combination of being a surgeon and a teenager was much more challenging than I had anticipated. But things didn't stay this way for long. A couple of weeks later, my Auntie Wei came over to my house. We had lunch together. Later, as we were sitting on my sofa, she turned to me and smiled, and then she carefully folded me into the shape of a sailboat. I had forgotten that Auntie Wei had recently become interested in origami.

I didn't last long as a sailboat, though. A week later, I morphed into a robot that could morph into a blue and white Ford Bronco 4x4 and from this Ford Bronco back to a robot again. That night, I went to dinner with some friends. I decided to go to the restaurant in my form as a robot. I was still Chinese, though. In fact, at the end of the night, when my friends began hugging each other goodbye, I morphed again—I grew spikes and curled up like an anteater so that no one could hug me goodbye. I generally do not like being hugged, much like others in my family. My grandmother also grows spikes and curls up into a ball every Christmas. I was ready to leave but then a few of my friends suggested that we all go clubbing, so I morphed into a blonde sixteen-year old girl with sparkling aquamarine eyes and a perfect size-six figure. However, once we got to the club, the security staff refused to let me in because I was only sixteen. I tried to flirt with them to win them over but all I discovered was that not many people use terms like "pash" or "will you go with me" anymore. It turned out that, not only were my schoolyard flirtation techniques from 1984 somewhat outdated, but I had been reading too many *Sweet Valley High* teen romance books as well. In the end, I gained entry into the club by morphing into Heather Locklear. I was still Chinese though—I was a Chinese version of Heather Locklear. I spent an hour or so at the club but, even though I soon became very popular, I knew that it wasn't my scene. I told my friends that I was leaving and then I grew some spikes again and I took the last tram home.

Back at my house, I stood in my living room and reflected on the events of the last few weeks. In particular, I thought about morphing. As I looked down at myself and the form I was currently in—a Chinese version of Heather Locklear with some spikes—I wondered if I should reconsider my approach to morphing. According to various myths and popular stories, morphing is sometimes accomplished via touch: "whatever you touch, you become." I picked up my television remote control and I thought about that idea for a moment. I hadn't realized that morphing could be so tactile, but maybe that was what I needed to incorporate better into my morphing: touching.

At any rate, as I switched on the television, I felt certain of at least one thing: sometimes, morphing is tiring. This was why I decided that, for now, the morphing rule could be changed to "whatever you watch, you become." So it was no wonder that, as I relaxed by watching some random early-morning TV programs, I began to morph into a kind of infomercial cyborg— half-human, half-home-fitness-system.

2. *Look Who's Morphing Too*

There was a word-processing operator who became part of a company restructure. There was a teenage basketballer who became a werewolf. There was an auntie who was possessed by a demon.

Me, I morphed into Dr. Quinn from the television show *Dr. Quinn, Medicine Woman*, all ready for my lunch date that day with Tara. I thought that becoming Dr. Quinn would make me Tara's ultimate sexual fantasy. After I had morphed into Dr. Quinn, I looked at myself in my bathroom mirror and smiled with satisfaction at how pretty I looked. Although my blue dress was in the style of the American Wild West period and it was a bit boring, I still looked beautiful in every other respect. I especially liked my long and lustrous brown hair. Eventually, after I had finished looking at myself, I drove to the seafood restaurant where Tara and I were to have our date. When I walked into the restaurant, I saw that Tara was already waiting at a table for me. Smiling, I approached her. Naturally, she did not recognise me at first, but after a while I managed to explain to her who I was. Unfortunately, once Tara had absorbed the news that I had morphed into Dr. Quinn, she was not as happy as I had hoped and in fact she declared that she could no longer be attracted to me. I said that I had a lot more than Dr. Quinn in me and to prove it I morphed into John Gielgud, distinguished thespian and one of the greatest Shakespearean actors of all time. More precisely, I was a young Gielgud, and I was wearing the black princely robes of Gielgud's costume from the 1934 West End production of *Hamlet* at the New Theatre. Tara cried out in recognition. She took a step toward me but I did not stay as Gielgud's Hamlet for long. I wanted to show Tara more of my range so I morphed into the construction worker from the Village People. I had on a white hard hat and ripped, faded jeans. I grinned at her as I rolled up my shirtsleeves. Tara liked what she saw so she morphed into a man who was wearing a leather cap and leather jeans and I knew then that everything was going to be all right with us. We decided to skip lunch and instead drove straight to my place to have sex, me as the construction worker from the Village People and her as the man who was wearing a leather cap and leather jeans. We were already kissing each other frantically as I opened the front door. Tara wanted sex very badly. She told me that she had never done it with an Asian guy who had morphed into Dr. Quinn from *Dr. Quinn, Medicine Woman,* then into Gielgud's Hamlet from the 1934 West End production at the New Theatre and then into the construction worker from the Village People before.

However, as Tara clutched at my shirt while kissing me, I suddenly morphed again—or, more specifically, my desires morphed. I led Tara to my living room and I told her to lie down on the rug. I then lay beside her and kissed her roughly, slipping my hands under her white T-shirt. Tara liked what I was doing and soon she pushed my hands down to her leather jeans. As I unbuttoned her jeans, I told her about morphing. I said that, according to various myths and popular stories, morphing is sometimes accomplished via touch: "whatever you touch, you become." Then I declared that I was going to show her some more of these myths and stories, and how powerfully they could work. Tara reached out to run her hand over the front of my tight workman's shirt. Moaning into my ear, she told me that, although that sounded really hot and she was happy to do as much touching as possible, she was not in the mood to read any short story collections or books of mythology right now. However, I simply smiled at her and I reassured her that that was no problem because the myths and popular stories were also on television. Upon hearing this, Tara looked at me with great joy, and then even greater lust. I picked up my television remote control and I rolled on top of her. I felt her wrap her leather-clad legs around me. As I switched on the television, I told her that, for now, the morphing rule would be changed to "whatever you watch, you become." So it was no wonder that, as Tara and I watched my favourite daytime television program while having sex, we soon morphed again, this time changing into Bo and Hope from *Days of Our Lives*.

3. Look Who's Morphing Now

There was a telemarketer who shape-shifted into a blood-sucking aristocrat one London night. There was a Chinese woman who got a perm. There was a sea sponge that, over millions of years, developed into a human.

Me, I migrated to Australia with my parents and my brother, and I immediately began morphing into various celebrities. On my very first day in Australia, I decided to morph into Barbra Streisand. The next morning, while eating breakfast with my family, I surprised them by morphing into Richard Simmons. I lived as Richard Simmons for a week but I realized that being a fitness celebrity just wasn't me, so I morphed into Princess Diana. By this stage, I had become more aware of the difficulties of adjusting to a new life in Australia, so I decided to stay as Princess Diana for a while—if only so that I could have some stability. But, a few days later, I changed my mind and became Liberace. Not everyone approved of my morphing. In fact, when I started morphing, some people said that it was a shame that I had become so westernized and that I should do more to retain my culture. As a result of these comments, my parents enrolled me in a language school that ran Cantonese lessons every Saturday morning. As Liberace, I would arrive at the language school each week in my glittering Volkswagen Beetle with a customised Rolls Royce hood. Before class began, I would take off my cape with a flourish and a stagehand would put the cape in my Beetle. The stagehand would then drive the Beetle away with my cape in it and return to put the cape on me at the conclusion of each lesson. I would say a few parting words to my classmates and teacher in Cantonese and be driven away. After a few weeks of this, I became the most popular person in my class and even my parents were moderately pleased with my success at the language school.

However, despite my success at my Cantonese lessons, my parents had another concern. My brother Hank had adjusted to our family's migration to Australia in a different way than I. He was morphing into members of bands like Mötley Crüe, KISS, and Poison. Although his appearance changed greatly as a result, it was neither his long, teased hair nor his very tight denim jeans nor his heavy use of stage makeup that concerned my parents. Instead, my parents had begun to worry about the debauched lifestyle that he was leading. He was staying out all night to indulge in sexual promiscuity, substance abuse, fights with his band mates, and property damage. My parents declared that, even though migration to a vastly different country was a major change for any person, Hank had taken the idea of morphing much too far.

One afternoon, Hank came home as usual, and my parents and I noticed straight away that he had morphed again. He had left the house that morning as Bon Scott from AC/DC but now he looked different. He was shirtless and wearing leather pants and a top hat. His hair was long and curly and he was smoking a cigarette. He mumbled a hello to us and then walked straight into his bedroom. My parents turned to me and asked who Hank was supposed to be. I identified him as Slash, the former lead guitarist of Guns N' Roses. At that point, my parents walked straight into Hank's room and angrily told him that they did not like the directions in which his life was going. An argument occurred but, after a while, I stepped in and dealt with the situation. I assured my parents that Hank's morphing was not so unusual. In fact, I told them that, in Australia, Hank's morphing could possibly be considered normal behaviour for a young male. This knowledge gladdened my parents somewhat and they even apologized to Hank for entering his room uninvited and we all smiled at each other in relief. We then decided to enjoy a nice family dinner together.

While my mother and Hank prepared the dinner, my father and I had a chat on the sofa in the living room. As my father handed me a beer, he confessed to me that, while it was reassuring to know that Hank was mostly normal and that I was doing well in my Cantonese lessons, all of this morphing was making life a lot more difficult for our family. He said that he would feel much better about the morphing if it didn't have to make things quite so stressful and uncertain. In response, I told my father that I too had been thinking about morphing. I said that, according to various myths and popular stories, morphing is sometimes accomplished via touch: "whatever you touch, you become." At first, my father seemed fascinated by this information. Then he looked warily at the tuxedo suit I was wearing. It was a classic Liberace outfit—a rhinestone-studded suit with designs of piano keyboards glittering on the wide jacket lapels. He asked me if touching my jacket would turn him into Liberace, but I shook my head and said it was unlikely. I declared that, as quick and easy as that particular process of morphing seemed, the majority of these myths and stories ultimately suggested that morphing was difficult and complex. In particular, the morphing that occurred in these tales sometimes resulted in further, unexpected changes—not only for the person who morphed but also for those they cared about most. Upon hearing this news, my father looked pained. When I saw the look on his face, I felt sad myself. I told him that if it was any consolation, the Greco-Roman gods and their associates had far more troubling issues with morphing than our family was currently having. I went on to relate the tale of Marsyas, who was part-man, part-goat. One day, Marsyas challenged the god Apollo to a flute-playing contest, but he lost. Afterward, the victorious Apollo sought to punish Marsyas for his hubris in challenging a god, so he killed Marsyas by skinning him alive. Upon hearing this story, my father looked horrified. But then I told him that, although Marsyas's passage into death was dramatic and brutal, perhaps the most significant act of morphing occurred afterward, when Marsyas's family and friends wept over his death. They wept so long and hard that their tears drenched the earth. At first, these tears formed a little stream, but eventually they transformed into a river. After he had heard this, my father did not say anything. He just looked sadder than ever. When I saw my father's face, I didn't feel like doing any more story telling. For a moment, he and I simply looked at each other. Although my father and I have rarely showed any affection toward each other, I decided to reach out to him. As I touched his shoulder in sympathy, I felt something within me change: I came to a new conclusion about the morphing in our family. At that point, my mother and Hank entered the room. They were carrying plates with our dinner served up— beef with black bean sauce using the traditional recipe that has been passed down from generation to generation within our family. My father got up from the sofa to take his usual place at the dining room table. Since our family had recently fallen into the habit of eating dinner with the television on, I picked up the television remote control from the coffee table. As I did this, I thought about the new conclusion that I had come to: although morphing—and its associated difficulties— was inevitable in our family, if I could make things easier for them for even a brief period, that had to be better than nothing. Feeling a little better, I joined my family at the dining table and we began to eat. As I switched on the television, I turned to my father and smiled at him. I said that I had decided that, for the next half hour, the morphing rule would be changed to "whatever you watch, you become." So it was no wonder that, as we watched repeats of our favourite family television show, we all morphed together. Eating our perfect family dinner, we happily changed into the family from *The Cosby Show*.

COCK ROCK

One clear and sunny afternoon, I rampaged through Tokyo, just as Godzilla had always done. However, I had not morphed into Godzilla or any other kind of giant reptilian creature. I was simply myself, except that I was fifty-five metres tall with a commensurate degree of physical strength and I had atomic ray breath and I was wearing a leather vest with blue stonewash jeans that were tucked into leopard-skin platform boots and I had a giant electric guitar slung across my back and I had a guitar amplifier clipped to my belt.

Concentrating my attack upon central Tokyo, I made my way through its busiest streets. I had never been to Tokyo before but this did not detract from my enjoyment in wreaking destruction. I fired my atomic ray breath at billboards for movies and clothes and perfumes, instantly incinerating their glamorous images. I punched giant holes into high-rise office buildings and watched them collapse. Each footstep I took involved the destruction of property. As I listened to the sound of vehicles and monuments being crushed beneath my platform boots, I smiled. The sun was shining upon me and I felt as pleased as a child who is jumping into puddles.

The people of Tokyo had been living in fear of Godzilla since 1954, and they had even experienced an attack by Alice Cooper in 1990, but they had never had the experience of me rampaging through their city. Most of the citizens reacted in a relatively traditional way by screaming in terror and fleeing. I looked down, watching as they ran away from me. They were dispersing in all directions, without regard for traffic signals or the presence of nearby pedestrian crossings. However, some people were too fascinated by my presence to flee. These people stood and pointed at me, remarking on my clothes and some of my other features, such as my huge fists and powerful legs. I felt quite appreciative of this. Even as I was destroying major buildings and landmarks in their city, these citizens were taking the time to comment on my great strength and power. At one point, I noticed a man who seemed especially fascinated by me. He was standing on the footpath outside a cinema, just a few metres away from my left foot. I saw him shake his head in awe and cry out "Wow—how tall is that guy!" so I paused in my rampage and smiled down at him and proudly told him that I was exactly fifty-five metres tall. However, the man informed me that he had been posing a rhetorical question and thus—as has happened to me so many times in my life—I realized that I had taken his comment too literally. I wanted to cover my embarrassment, so I changed the topic by destroying part of a building: I turned to my right, saw what looked to be a luxury hotel and tried to look busy as I punched a hole into its penthouse level. As I stomped away, I cursed myself for my tendency to create conversational mishaps by being so literal-minded. Such mishaps seem to happen to me with embarrassing regularity. Yet, as I bemoaned this tendency, I could not help wondering why it was that I could be so literal sometimes and so immersed in fantasy at other times. Interestingly, as well as having a tendency to be overly literal,

I can sometimes be overly analytical. Thus, as I continued my rampage, I decided to ruminate upon my attraction to the world of fantasy and the world of the literal. As I paused to tread on a row of buses at a bus terminal, I asked myself: Am I drawn to the world of the literal because of its apparent certainties, its sense of organization and structure? Then, as I fired my atomic ray breath at the remaining buses that were speeding away, I asked myself: Am I drawn to the world of fantasy for the very opposite reason—because it has less structure and can seem so elastic in nature? Turning away to punch a glass-fronted office building, I also wondered: Do we spend our lives managing the tensions between these two worlds of fantasy and the literal? As I watched the fractured glass panels from the building crash onto the street, I felt compelled to pose the question: What would an experience that perfectly combines fantasy and the literal look like?

However, I soon realized that I did not have the time to contemplate such matters further. This was because I had noticed some fighter jets flying toward me. Then I heard a rumbling sound below me. Looking back down to the street, I frowned as I saw a column of armoured tanks approaching. I waited until the tanks and jets had closed in and then I stomped on the tanks while punching the fighter jets out of the sky. As I did this, I could not help but feel annoyed by the predictability of the Japanese government's actions in sending the military after me. It irked me that the government—this institution of power—had issued such a banal response. As well as being a potential violation of Japan's post-war pacifist constitution, the government's response was lacking in vision. After all, surely the tactic of sending the military after me would only serve to provoke me? Certainly, the more fighter jets that I punched away and the more tanks that I crushed under my boots, the more annoyed and bored I became.

Thus, as soon as I had dealt with the jets and tanks, I decided to engage in one of the world's greatest methods of demonstrating contempt for authority and tedium: I swung my electric guitar around to the front of my body, took a cable from my back pocket, plugged my guitar into my amplifier, stood with my legs apart, raised my right arm in the air, yelled "Tokyo! Are you ready to rock?" and brought my arm down to strike a loud and ringing guitar chord. After letting the chord reverberate for a few moments, I began to play rock music. I started playing one of my favourite guitar moments: the opening of Mötley Crüe's "Kickstart My Heart" where the guitar sounds like an accelerating engine. Then I switched to the classic guitar riff for David Bowie's "Rebel Rebel," humming each note as I played it. At this point, I looked down and noticed that a crowd of people was gathering around me to watch and cheer me on. As I launched into one of the most played guitar riffs of all time—Deep Purple's "Smoke on the Water" riff—I also noticed that many people were no longer fleeing from me but were now running back toward me. Encouraged, I played famous guitar riffs from more rock songs and this prompted more cheering and more people joining the crowd, and then I played and sang whole songs, and the crowd grew in a very big way and they also became quite excited and they sang along, and this encouraged me even more, and also drew further masses of people to join the crowd to cheer and sing and shake their heads in time with the music and, soon enough, the people of Tokyo were partying as one to the sounds of my rock guitar virtuosity and vocal mastery.

Thus began an epic rock concert that went on into the night. An enormous PA system was flown in by helicopters and set up for me. A giant cluster of microphones was attached to a nearby office tower, positioned at the height of my mouth. Towering amplifier stacks were placed behind me. I discarded my battery-powered amplifier and plugged my guitar into the new set-up. Smiling, I called out for the volume to be turned up to eleven. Then I performed hit after hit, sending the crowd into a state of ecstasy. They looked up at me—some of them peering through binoculars—and they sang along with every song. They danced and crowd-surfed to the faster songs. They held up their lighters in the air for the power ballads. As I saw the many lighter flames glowing below me, I sighed and told the crowd how beautiful they looked. At various points during the concert, the crowd even did the Mexican Wave. The people could not get enough of me. The chanting of my name echoed through the city. I spotted signs being held up amongst the crowd, telling me in both English and Japanese how much I was loved. Girls wept. I sang and played my way through many highlights of the western rock music canon. I covered almost every form of rock I could think of, including hard rock, glam rock, punk rock, grunge, surf rock, rockabilly, rock 'n' roll, psychedelic rock, and heavy metal. As the sun went down, lighting rigs were set up next to me. I smiled in satisfaction as I looked all around me, taking in the sight of the massive crowd illuminated under the night sky. I was hot and sweating, and my perspiration was raining down onto the crowd, but they did not mind this at all. In fact, some of the girls in the crowd squealed with delight as my sweat poured down upon them. When I could not think of any more songs to play, the crowd screamed out song requests for me. Interestingly, most of the songs that the crowd requested were "cock rock" hits by hard rock and glam metal bands whose music I had grown up with. As a result, I ended up performing songs such as KISS's "I Was Made for Lovin' You," Bon Jovi's "Livin' on a Prayer," and even Warrant's "Cherry Pie." These songs prompted me to strut around and show off my guitar techniques more than ever. The more I played these songs, the more I grew in confidence. Since cock rock lyrics often describe sexual encounters and use a great deal of sexual double-entendre, I became emboldened enough to make suggestive sexual moves with my guitar. I stroked my hand up and down the guitar's neck and thrust my guitar toward the audience and gyrated with it. The crowd loved these moves and I realized that I loved performing them too, and as a result, this part of the concert went on for quite some time.

As the night went on, the crowd's passion for the music seemed endless but, eventually, I became tired. When an unexpected chant arose from the crowd calling upon me to play Queen's "Bohemian Rhapsody," I knew that it was time for me to wind up the concert. Deciding that "Bohemian Rhapsody" would be a powerful end to my show, I performed the entire song. Once I had sung the song's closing lines, I waved to the crowd wearily and yelled out, "Thank you, Tokyo! Thank you and goodnight!" Everyone cheered but then they continued to cheer and soon they were calling out, "More! More!" It was then that I realized that I had forgotten about encores. So I performed what turned out to be three long, sweaty and very exhausting encores. Finally, after making it all the way through the crowd's request for Led Zeppelin's "Stairway to Heaven," then performing the crowd's subsequent request for a cock rock version of Don McLean's "American Pie," and then finally acquiescing to the crowd's demand that I perform a medley of songs from Meat Loaf's *Bat Out of Hell* album, I took off my guitar, raised it above my head in tired triumph, looked out across the massive crowd and said my final goodbye for the evening.

As I walked away from the cluster of microphones, the crowd gradually parted to let me through. I glanced down at my feet and saw some of the concert-goers reaching out to touch my platform boots as I passed by. Looking all around me, I saw masses of people slowly dispersing and leaving the area. Some especially persistent fans followed me and called out my name and said that they wanted me to keep performing but some pretty girls in the crowd said, "Shush. Let him sleep." Eventually, I was left alone. I stumbled out of the city centre and I kept walking, heading further away from the noise of the crowd and out into the suburbs. After a while, I came across a large, deserted park. This park looked like a nice place to rest for the night. It had manicured lawns, neat flower gardens and pretty cherry trees. I walked into the centre of the park, took my guitar off and laid it on the grass. I gently sat myself down on the lawn and slowly stretched my body out across the full length of the park. I lay back, resting my head on top of a large cluster of cherry trees, and I stared up at the stars, absorbing what had happened, and soon fell asleep.

When I awoke, it was daylight. I felt the sun shining on my skin and I slowly opened my eyes. It was another clear and sunny day. I was not sure how much time had passed since I had fallen asleep but it seemed that I had been in a deep sleep for at least eight hours. I attempted to rise. However, I was not able to do so. In fact, I found that I could not move any part of my body except for my head. I realized with shock that my entire body from the shoulders down was fastened to the ground. I could feel ropes against my torso and limbs and, craning my head as far as I could, I saw that all of these ropes were attached to giant stakes that were firmly anchored into the ground. I struggled against the ropes but it was no use—I could barely move. I felt almost ill with fear.

Then I heard a mechanical noise near my left ear. I turned my head to the side and saw a forklift truck parked right beside my shoulder. Resting on the prongs of the forklift was a rising platform and standing on that platform was a pretty girl. This girl, who looked like she was in her early twenties, was wearing a short black skirt and a red tank top. The platform rose to the height of my shoulder and then I watched as the girl stepped off the platform and onto my shoulder. She waved at me and smiled and skipped about on my shoulder, her little skirt fluttering. She wandered down to my chest and laughed as she turned a few cartwheels. I looked at her in confusion and I thought about saying something to her, but then I heard the forklift operating again and I also heard some girlish giggling and I turned my head to see four more pretty girls standing on its platform. The platform stopped once again at my shoulder, and the girls squealed with joy and ran out onto my chest and joined the first girl. Together, they laughed and skipped about on my chest. Then I heard the forklift operating again. I looked toward my left shoulder to see four more girls standing on its rising platform. I began to feel panicky. I struggled helplessly against my bindings once again.

Soon, there were twenty girls running around on my chest. All of these girls were very pretty. A few of them had their hair up, but most wore their long hair loose. While many of the girls were wearing short skirts and summer tops, a few were wearing other types of outfits. Some of the younger girls—who looked to be in their twenties—were wearing cheerleading outfits. Another—who looked to be in her forties—appeared to have come to the park straight from her workplace. Her short black business skirt and cream-coloured blouse suggested that she worked in a corporate environment. The youngest-looking—who seemed to be in her late teens—wore a navy blue sailor-style school dress and carried a school satchel. I nervously asked the girls what they were doing on my body but, gushing to me in English, they interrupted to tell me how much they loved my music. They talked in awed tones about how well I had performed songs such as Warrant's "Cherry Pie" and KISS's "I Was Made for Lovin' You." I hesitated for a moment but then I told the girls that I really wasn't as good a musician as they thought. I confessed that I was primarily a covers guitarist who happened to know some rock guitar clichés and who could also do a bit of soloing on the minor pentatonic scale. However, the girls interrupted to gush to me that I was so big and strong and handsome and they were my greatest fans ever. Then they sighed and told me that they loved me and they wandered down my chest. I felt them walk onto my stomach. They giggled as I squirmed under the ropes. They continued moving downwards, stepping onto a patch of skin that was exposed where my vest was open. A few of the girls were wearing stiletto heels and their footsteps felt like tiny pin pricks against my skin. I pleaded with all of the girls to tell me what they were doing. As they stepped up onto the waistband of my jeans, the girls told me that I was a sexy rock god and that they wanted to worship my body. I craned my head up once more and I saw that all of them had gathered around the top button of my jeans. As they worked together to slip the button out of its buttonhole, I sweated in panic. I told the girls that they had it all wrong: I may have performed some cock rock songs by bands like KISS, Bon Jovi, and Warrant, but I was not the confident "cock rock god" that those performances suggested. I paused and then I told them sadly that I was unlikely to live up to their expectations or my own. However, the girls just kept attending to my jeans. They finally undid the top button and gave a little squeal of joy. Then they turned their attention to my jeans zipper. As they slowly pulled my zipper downward, I felt more anxious than ever.

When my zipper was fully opened, I looked down at the girls. Their faces were flushed with excitement and they were telling me how much they wanted to worship my body. I begged them, "Please don't look in there. It's private." The girl who had first stepped onto my body looked up at me. She gave me a little smile and said "You're such a hottie," and she disappeared into my jeans. My body tensed up as she slipped into the fly of my briefs. I felt the shock of her touch on my bare skin. She began to explore me and, suddenly, she stopped. As her head emerged from the fly of my briefs, I looked down at her in fear. But she had only poked her head out of my briefs so that she could call out to the other girls: "Hey girls—what are you waiting for? Come on in."

I watched in disbelief as, one by one, the girls began entering my jeans and slipping into the fly of my briefs. As they filled up my briefs, I shifted a little under the ropes at their touch but my body remained tense. I looked on helplessly as the final girl prepared to enter my jeans. This was the girl who was wearing the sailor-style school dress. Just as she was about to disappear from view, this sailor-girl looked up at me and she said, "You know, I really think you should let yourself enjoy it. Sometimes you think too much." Then she giggled and joined the others.

The girls started to pleasure me. I was so nervous and scared. I was also disbelieving that they could see me as some kind of cock rock god. I wanted to ask them, "How can you believe in me this way? I do not even believe in myself this way." Yet, as I listened to the faint sounds of the girls sighing and cooing from inside my briefs, I felt unable to ask such questions. As a result, I said nothing as they continued to pleasure me. They touched me very gently at first, although their caresses gradually became stronger. I took a deep breath and I told myself to relax. I tried to reassure myself that I could be safe with these girls. After all, they were fans who adored me—they seemed to be loving fans, not unhealthily obsessed fans with murderous tendencies. Furthermore, despite my fear and awkwardness, I could sense a great deal of respect in their touch. After a while, I even became struck by the reverence of their touch. As

I listened to their sighs, I realized that these girls really were engaging in an act of worship—they truly were willing to see me as a cock rock god. In fact, as they continued to pleasure me, I wondered if the power of cocks—like the power of gods—is ultimately sustained by passion and belief. So I took another deep breath. I leaned my head back and I closed my eyes. The ropes held me so tightly. I began to feel the sensation and the sheer power and extravagance of having twenty girls worshipping me. After a while, I sweated. I became breathless. I moved against the ropes and I could hear sighing and cooing in response to this. Soon, my cock became hard. The girls immediately squealed in excitement. My cock got harder and harder and they squealed all the more. As I listened to their squeals, I could not help smiling. Finally, I really began to enjoy what was happening to me. The sensations produced by the girls spread throughout my body. As I enjoyed myself, I could not help but analyze my situation. For now at least, I had become a cock rock god, and I had twenty pretty girls who wanted to worship my body and these girls had literally gotten into my pants. This made me suspect that the moment that I was sharing with them was in fact an experience that perfectly combined fantasy and the literal. Although it may have constituted "thinking too much," I allowed myself the pleasure of this intellectualization before once again abandoning myself to the adoration that was being practiced by the girls.

Thus began various ceremonies of worship that went on for many hours. There was a light breeze, and the perfumes and colours of the park's flower gardens were all around us. It was spring in Japan—right in the middle of April—and the cherry blossoms were in full bloom. When I craned my head up, I could see cherry trees in the distance, near my feet. When I leaned my head back, the cherry blossom flowers under my head served as the softest pillow. In this setting, the girls and I worshipped and played, drifting in and out of states of ecstasy. As they touched me over and over, I knew that this park was not the place to hold back. The sun shone upon me and I let myself feel pleasure from every caress. The girls were the most devoted and fervent fans a cock rock god could want. As well as paying loving attention to my cock, they eagerly roamed over other parts of my body. They crawled under my vest and rubbed themselves against my nipples. They giggled as they splashed each other with the sweat that had accumulated in my navel. They sighed as they lovingly stroked the scar along my abdomen. In the end, the girls gave me so many variations of pleasure and I sent them back into my pants so many times, that my body shook and strained against the ropes over and over. Finally, when I had told them that I was sated for the time being, they made their way back to my stomach to rest. They looked beautifully sweaty and exhilarated. They were also completely covered with my come. As they wiped my come from their eyes, I looked at them with concern, but they laughed and reassured me that they were fine. They added that I was turning out to be quite the cock rock god. They even declared that, although technically I was not omnipresent as a deity, due to my height it did honestly seem to them as if I was everywhere at once. In response, I smiled and looked at them in wonder. These girls knew how to make me feel powerful and I loved them for this. I thanked them and then I announced that now

I had a surprise for them. I opened my mouth and I stuck my tongue right out—just like Gene Simmons from KISS—and the girls cried out in joy.

And so it was that, as the sun sank lower in the sky, I began to pleasure all twenty of my girls, giving them many blissful moments. I gazed at them lovingly and I asked all of them to come up to my lips so that I might kiss them, and they did: they sprinted up my body and threw themselves against my lips. They clustered together in groups so that I could kiss many of them at once. At first, I gave them soft, little kisses. Gradually, however, they became impatient and began throwing themselves against my lips, demanding that I stroke them with my tongue. I teased them for a while longer and then my tongue finally emerged from my mouth and I began to lick them all over. They cried out with pleasure. At that moment, my greatest desire was to be everywhere at once upon these girls' bodies, so I stroked them over and over, falling into a joyously familiar, almost-meditative state. I closed my eyes and inhaled deeply so that I could enjoy the scent of their arousal.

Eventually, I also sent the girls to other parts of my body to find pleasure. I curled my hands into fists and ordered successive groups of the girls to straddle my knuckles. Each group of girls rocked back and forth, rubbing themselves against the hard bones, panting at first and then making little moans and, eventually, groaning as they came. My cock was also hard again, so I told a few of the girls to ride it for as long as they wished. As these girls clapped their hands together in happiness and ran down to my cock, I told another group of girls to stay upon my stomach: this latter group were delighted when I instructed them to strip off their outer garments and to pleasure each other for as long as they wanted. Among them was the girl who was wearing corporate clothing. I took particular delight in witnessing her transformation as she unpinned her hair, shook it out of its bun, took off her glasses and stripped off her corporate attire to reveal a white lacy designer camisole that perfectly showed off the large curves of her body. Soon, she and the other girls in this group were frantically touching each other and the wetness from their beautiful cunts was dripping down onto my leather vest. As all of these scenes with my twenty girls continued, I looked down at my body and I smiled.

The hours passed as the girls and I continued to worship and play. During this time, I barely noticed the sun setting over Tokyo. I was too entranced by the ways that we were touching each other—and the stories that we went on to tell each other. At first, the girls sat on my stomach and we shared a few titillating anecdotes. Soon, however, we were confessing fantasy after fantasy, blushing with arousal and, at times, with shame. We told each other about arses that were as needy as cunts, mouths that were as needy as arses, rough sex in luxurious locations, boy-on-boy sex played out between girls, fantasies based upon hair colour, fantasies based upon skin colour, adult activities based upon childhood memories, adult activities based upon childlike behaviour, and sex scenes discovered in books and films as a child and replayed in adolescent masturbation over and over again. I told the girls that they could tell me whatever they wanted and touch themselves wherever they wanted and, after a while, their hands strayed under their skirts and dresses and soon the telling of their fantasies was accompanied by panting and moaning. I listened as the girls' narratives became increasingly fragmented and, a few minutes later, when all of them eagerly ran down toward my cock to continue their pleasure there, it seemed that the telling of their fantasies might stop altogether. However, I ordered four of the girls to go to my ears and I asked them to say whatever dirty and intimate things they wanted, touching themselves all the while. These girls soon complied and thus, as the other sixteen girls entered my briefs, I had a pair of girls at each ear, whispering filthy and loving sentiments to me in stereo.

As this intermingling of play and fantasy continued, the moon began to illuminate the city and the lights of the park were switched on. In all of this light, the girls' bodies cast shadows upon my own body. My body became a terrain for their imagination and pleasure as well as my own. Finally, after some hours had passed, the girls returned to lie on my stomach, sated and happy. They snuggled up together. I asked them if they wanted to sleep, but they said that they weren't quite ready to do this yet. Instead, they asked me to tell them some bedtime stories. At first, I wondered what stories I could relate, but I was soon telling them about the cock rock that I knew and its associated gods. I related story after story of number-one hits, controversial lyrics, disputes with record companies, failed solo careers, concept albums, comeback albums and greatest-hits albums. I interspersed this with tales of sexual promiscuity, substance abuse, fights with band mates, and property damage. I discussed the characterization of rock music as the Devil's music. I spoke at length about Mötley Crüe. Finally, I told them stories about how punk changed everything.

By the time I had finished telling all of these bedtime stories, the sky looked a little brighter. It was the early hours of the morning. I looked at the girls upon my stomach and I realized that, not only had I told them hours and hours of stories, but they did not look sleepy at all. Instead, their eyes were wide and bright and they were all sitting up with enraptured looks upon their faces. It was then that I realized that the stories I had chosen to tell them were not very suitable for inducing relaxation or sleepiness. I started to apologize but they interrupted me to tell me how much they loved my stories. They sighed with awe and then they declared me to be the world's greatest story teller.

When the girls saw how pleased I was with this comment, they told me a story of their own. This story was about the gods who existed before our world began. Rather than being interested in plagues and natural disasters, these gods were focused on one thing only: ecstasy. As a result, they spent many days and nights in the heavens, worshipping and playing with each other and listening to music and dancing and engaging in other forms of revelry, creating ecstasy before they created anything else. Eventually, these gods got around to creating the Earth. In the beginning, when they created the Earth, it was a world of arid rock that was unable to support any form of life. However, after this act of creation, they again engaged passionately in ritual after ritual of devotion and art-making and sexual play. All of the fluids of exertion and desire that were generated from these ecstatic activities flowed down from the heavens and onto the Earth, and these fluids rained down for many days, drenching the Earth until the gods had created the oceans of our world. These oceans provided the moisture that was necessary for life to exist. At first, only unicellular organisms—ancient forms of bacteria—populated the Earth. Over billions of years, as multicellular organisms developed, the first amphibians emerged from the oceans that the gods had created from their ecstasy. These amphibians diversified and evolved into many kinds of animals, including primates and the early ancestors of humans. The ancestors of humans walked hunched over but, gradually, humans began to walk upright, needing and searching for and sometimes creating forms of ecstasy, drawn to ecstasy with the sense that it might be an essential quality of existence, even if they remained unaware of its place as the world's original life force.

After this story was told, there was a moment of silence. As each girl bowed her head solemnly, immersed in her own thoughts, I thought about these gods that the girls had spoken of. It seemed to me that they were the original cock rock gods. In fact, the existence of these gods made me think that, in one sense, I was not really a cock rock god at all. Recalling the story that the girls had told me, I thought about how the original cock rock gods had to create ecstasy before they could create life itself. This suggested something fundamental about the place of ecstasy in the broader scheme of things. Thus, perhaps my duty, as symbolized by my own cock, was to search for and create ecstasy for myself and for others in the ways that were available to me—to be an envoy, if you like, for the original cock rock gods. These forms of ecstasy could certainly involve sexual ecstasy but were not necessarily limited to this—after all, as demonstrated by the gods' original revelries and my own concert the night before, ecstasy could be found in other realms, such as art. In fact, it seemed that ecstasy could be found in many forms that I was yet to conceive of or experience. Did all of this mean, then, that I needed to broaden my concept of cock?

Yet, just at that point, my ruminations were interrupted by some excited cries from the girls. I looked down and saw the sailor-girl closing her school satchel. She looked back at me and took a deep breath. She declared that, besides me, there was at least one more cock rock god in this park. At that point, she boldly lifted up her skirt, revealing her own cock, held in place by leather straps. The sailor-girl giggled at the look of shock on my face. She declared to me that, while she did not have a penis, sometimes she had a cock. As I continued to stare at the little sailor-girl and her very big cock, I could only nod in response. I had not expected that my concept of cock would be broadened quite so soon, nor in quite this way.

The sailor-girl strutted about on my stomach with her cock, playfully flashing her skirt up and down, and swaggering around like Mick Jagger in concert. Soon she made her way over to one of the girls who was wearing a cheerleader's uniform. The sailor-girl grinned and winked at her. The cheerleader gave her a knowing smile, her eyes darting down to the sailor-girl's cock. The sailor-girl caressed the cheerleader's face for a moment, then she turned her around, bent her over, kicked her feet apart, grabbed onto her curvaceous hips, and began fucking her from behind with her cock. The cheerleader moaned and, after a while, her fists clenched and her eyes widened and her face took on an expression that seemed poised between agony and pleasure. Eventually, she was coming hard and crying out. After she finished coming, she unclenched her fists but the sailor-girl kept fucking her, just as hard as before, and the cheerleader moaned helplessly and soon she was coming again. As I watched all of this, my initial shock about the sailor-girl was gradually replaced with admiration. What an astonishing figure this sailor-girl was—so pretty and so powerful a cock rock god. Beyond this, I felt awed by her audacity. It occurred to me that maybe a certain level of audacity is required to claim one's place as a cock rock god. At the very least, it seemed that audacity had great potential to facilitate experiences of ecstasy. I considered articulating these thoughts to the other eighteen girls but, when I looked around at them, I noticed that they were very preoccupied with looking at the sailor-girl's crotch. Soon enough, all of these girls had formed a line in front of the sailor-girl. They knelt before her, more than ready to receive her cock in any way that she chose to present it to them.

As she moved from girl to girl, the sailor-girl stroked her mighty cock. Her girls gazed at her with desire, some of them frantically touching themselves as they watched her. I watched with fascination as this scene took place. Soon, I felt myself becoming turned on. In fact, I found myself wishing that I owned porn that was this good. After a while, the sailor-girl looked up at me. She saw that I was aroused and this sight pleased her so she winked at me and sent ten of the girls to tend to my cock.

However, upon entering my briefs, these ten girls did not steadily and insistently stroke my cock as I expected them to. Instead, at the orders of the sailor-girl, they giggled and gave me teasing, intermittent caresses. As the sailor-girl continued to play with her other nine girls, I felt my arousal build. On the one hand, I found that I could not stop looking at the sailor-girl and her feats of cock rock godliness. On the other hand, the sight of the sailor-girl was making my cock was so achingly hard that I needed it to be properly stroked so that I could come. However, when I told the sailor-girl that I wanted to come, she just laughed. She told me that I had to be a good boy and wait. I looked at her in disbelief but she continued to play with her other girls. I sighed and decided that I could wait a little longer. I tried to remain as still as I could but, after some time, I did not feel that I could wait any more. Again, I asked her if she would let me come. This time, not only the sailor-girl but all of the other girls giggled at me, and things continued on as before. As I felt the girls in my briefs give my cock a few teasing, frustratingly soft caresses, I cried out with frustration—and a growing sense of anger. I silently willed the girls—any or all of them—to stroke my cock properly. But it was apparent that this was not going to happen for now. I clenched and unclenched my fists. I told the sailor-girl that I was becoming angry. The sailor-girl waggled a finger at me and gave me a little smile. She told me that good boys should wait and show some manners unless they want to get bad boy reputations.

Upon hearing this last comment, I groaned and strained furiously against the ropes, staring at the sailor-girl and her cock all the while. I felt the ropes pressing against my body, holding me in place as I tried to arch my back against them. The sailor-girl smiled as she watched me pushing against the ropes while taking in the sight of her. Excited and angered all the more by the sailor-girl's smile, I could hear my own breath coming faster as I met her gaze. Finally, as I gave a loud groan, the sailor-girl gently slipped her cock out of the mouth of one of the girls who was kneeling before her and she started walking up my stomach and, as she finally ordered the ten girls at my cock to begin stroking me properly, my eyes closed, and I felt her advancing up my chest and up the delicate skin of my neck and then she stepped onto my chin and onto my bottom lip and I gasped with shock at myself but I opened my mouth to let her slip inside me, cock and all.

Feeling the sailor-girl inside my mouth and the caresses of the girls at my cock, I strained against the ropes as hard as I could. After a little while, I detected a slight loosening in the ropes around my shoulders and biceps. Feeling a new sense of excitement, I continued to thrash around. As the ropes loosened still more, I found that I was able to lift part of my right shoulder off the park lawn. Once the nineteen girls on my body realized that the ropes were coming loose, they cried out in fear. Although their cries served to turn me on all the more, I now realized that, above all, I wanted to be free of the ropes that were restraining me. I opened my eyes to see the nine girls on my stomach clutching onto the edges of my leather vest. Then I heard the girls in my briefs screaming to me that I was going to come soon and begging me to not struggle so. However, I continued to struggle and I soon felt some give in the ropes around my hips. I closed my eyes again, feeling the pleasure from my cock inevitably build. As I experienced more and more ecstasy, the ropes began to fall away from me. I kicked them off my feet. I moved my left arm so that I could clutch onto some nearby trees. I gasped for breath and then I started to come. My body shook. I kept my eyes closed but I felt opened up all over.

Eventually, my body stopped shaking. Although I could still feel my heart beating strongly, my breath began to slow. As I opened my eyes and squinted into the morning sun, I felt the sailor-girl climb out of my mouth. She stepped out onto my bottom lip and slowly made her way back to my chest. Her hair and skin and dress were soaked with my saliva and she walked rather unsteadily at first but she seemed otherwise unharmed. Upon reaching my chest, she turned around to look at me. At first, I could not meet her eyes. I did not want to think about what she thought of me. I continued to avert my eyes but, eventually, when I realized that I needed to return her gaze, I saw that she was simply looking at me lovingly. For a moment, we stared at each other in silence.

I then looked down the length of my body. Most of the ropes were no longer on my torso. I looked around the sides of my body and I saw that many of the stakes that surrounded me were now askew and some had even been uprooted from the ground. At first, I smiled at this sight. But as I felt some of the girls emerging from my briefs, I suddenly remembered that, the sailor-girl aside, there had been nineteen other girls on my body—including nine who had squealed in terror and clung to my vest as I thrashed about. I quickly counted the number of girls who were on my body. I gave a thankful sigh as I realized that all twenty of them were present and unharmed. Yet, despite my relief, I could not help feeling guilty that I had frightened and shaken these girls so much. I knew that I had not intended to scare them—well, not that much. I looked down and apologized to them. However, as it turned out, they were not that frightened after all. The girls reminded me that Japan is one of the most earthquake-prone countries in the world, and they told me that the movements of my body against the ropes were not as bad as the earthquake tremors they had experienced. Then they sighed with lust and declared that they loved the way that I had bucked and thrust my body so powerfully against the ropes. Upon hearing this latter comment, I could not help blushing a little, even though I was an almighty cock rock god. However, they kindly ignored my blushing.

At that point, the nineteen girls began walking back to my chest to join the sailor-girl there. Soon, all the girls lay upon my chest, relaxing once more as I too lay back and relaxed. As they yawned and stretched, I gazed upon them with love and adoration. I told them what special girls they were. I thanked them for revealing so much about cocks—and my own cock in particular—to me. They declared that it had been their absolute pleasure. I reached down to them with my right hand and I gently caressed their bodies with the tip of my index finger. Smiling, I told them that it was time for all of us to get some sleep. Feeling mightier than King Kong, I tenderly scooped up all of the girls into the palms of my hands. I slowly sat up and brought them closer to my face. They looked beautifully and happily exhausted. Their clothes were stained with both their fluids and mine. Their hair was also in great disarray. At that point, I became aware that there was a gigantic patch of wetness under my arse and thighs, drenching the earth below me.

I looked at the girls and I thought about what we had done and I felt good. Bringing my hands to my lips, I kissed them very softly and I let my breath fall gently upon them. They swooned a little and smiled at me sleepily. I laid back and I placed the girls on my chest again. They lay on my chest in a row and I wished them sweet dreams and they quickly fell asleep. I then stared up at the sky, absorbing what had happened, and soon fell asleep too.

Later that afternoon, after my girls and I had slept, I played my farewell concert for the people of Tokyo. I returned to the city area where I had previously performed and everyone was there waiting for me. I strutted out in front of the massive crowd and I plugged in my guitar and I adopted my best cock rock god pose in front of my cluster of microphones. I opened the concert with one of my absolute cock rock favourites—Van Halen's "Hot for Teacher"—and the crowd screamed with joy. Right from the beginning of the song, I launched into my best Eddie Van Halen two-handed guitar techniques while prancing around like David Lee Roth. The crowd gave a roaring cheer that echoed throughout central Tokyo. Once I had finished this song, I launched into a song that I had listened to over and over as a child: "48 Crash," a song from one of the less-acknowledged cock rock gods, Suzi Quatro. I strutted about like Suzi and, toward the end of the song, I stuck my tongue right out and showed it to all of the girls in the crowd and they swooned with desire. As the song came to a close, I felt some tugging on the bottom of my jeans. Looking down, I saw that quite a few girls were clinging to the cuffs. They were trying to climb up my legs. As a crew of security guards removed them and dragged them back into the crowd, the girls looked up at me and we smiled at each other. After the last girl was pulled away from me to be returned to the crowd, I looked out at everyone and announced that now I was going to play one of the quintessential Australian cock rock songs. I played the opening notes of AC/DC's "You Shook Me All Night Long" and the crowd cried out in delight. As I performed this hit, the people of Tokyo sang along with every word. Midway through the song, I broke into an extended guitar solo. I thrust my guitar toward the audience and gyrated wildly with it. My solo continued for at least forty-five minutes, but the crowd loved every note that I played and every gyration that I made. Eventually, I got so caught up in my performance that, after I had finished my solo, I stripped off my leather vest and threw it out into the northern suburbs of Tokyo, and the crowd screamed their approval.

My concert continued throughout the afternoon and then into the night, when the lights were switched on. Throughout it all, the crowd remained just as passionate and ecstatic as the last time that I had performed for them. They called out song after song for me to play. I gave them every cock-rocking song they wanted, including hits by Guns N' Roses, Aerosmith, Poison, and Def Leppard. It also seemed appropriate for me to perform songs by James Brown, Jimi Hendrix, and Jerry Lee Lewis. Finally, when I gyrated my hips and launched into "Hound Dog," the crowd gave the biggest roar of all.

Eventually, however, I announced that it was time for me to go. Naturally, the crowd screamed out for more so I played four encores. Once I had finished all of my encores, I took my guitar off and I began destroying it by smashing it into some nearby buildings. As the buildings collapsed and chunks of concrete and steel fell down upon the people below, the crowd screamed with delight and fear. I then turned to another part of the street and smashed my guitar against the buildings there, prompting further joy and terror from the crowd. Finally, I slammed my guitar into a red illuminated billboard that was below me, producing a dissonant and deafening chord. Then I raised my guitar and I flung it as hard as I could. I watched with satisfaction as my guitar went flying and landed somewhere in Tokyo's outer eastern suburbs—this time, with a giant crash that made the ground shake. The crowd roared and cheered. I fired my atomic ray breath into the sky, raised my fist in the air in tired triumph and yelled out, "Thank you, Tokyo! Thank you and goodnight!"

Having said my goodbye to the people of Tokyo, I walked away from the spot where I had been performing. The crowd sighed with disappointment at first, but they gradually parted to let me through. In fact, as I made my way through the crowd, everyone was soon clapping and yelling out their support for me. The chanting of my name echoed through the city. I spotted signs being held up amongst the crowds, telling me how much I was loved. Girls wept.

Eventually, I made my way through the crowd until no one was left and I was walking alone. I walked out of the city centre and then through the busy inner city area, stomping through some of Japan's most fashionable urban districts. I trampled through some of Tokyo's suburbs, stepping on libraries, prestigious private schools, and well-kept gardens. Finally, I stomped out of Tokyo.

Travelling further and further away from the lights of the city, I walked toward the coast. I was being drawn to the water—and, like Godzilla after a rampage, I wanted to return to the island on which I lived. After a while, I came across a coastal highway. I followed this highway for a little while and, eventually, I arrived at a beach.

As I stepped onto the sand, I paused, looking out to the ocean. The beach was deserted and all that could be heard was the sound of the waves. I smiled. I walked toward the water.

Then I disappeared back into the sea.

ACKNOWLEDGMENTS

▼

Earlier versions of parts of this book first appeared in: *Adventures in Pop Culture, Antipodes, Best Australian Stories 2007, Cornerfold, Going Down Swinging, Griffith Review, HEAT, Meanjin, The New Quarterly*, and *Verandah*.

"Nagasaki"
Words by Mort Dixon, Music by Harry Warren
© 1928 (Renewed) Four Jays Music Co. and Olde Clover Leaf Music
(Administered by Bug Music)
All Rights Reserved
Used by Permission

The author does not intend to suggest that the creators of the song "Nagasaki", Harry Warren and Mort Dixon, were in any way responsible for or their song directly related to the 1945 bombing of Nagasaki. Reprinted with permission on behalf of Harry Warren by Four Jays Music Publishing.

This project is supported by the Victorian Government through Arts Victoria.

Much of this book was brought to fruition while I was supported with a Deakin University Postgraduate Research Scholarship as a doctoral candidate at Deakin University. I am also grateful for the support I received from the Australia Council for the Arts, Arts Victoria, and the University of Melbourne, where I was the 2001 DJ (Dinny) O'Hearn Memorial Fellow at The Australian Centre.

Special thanks for this edition of *Look Who's Morphing* to: Larissa Lai, Brian Lam and Robert Ballantyne of Arsenal Pulp Press, Glad Day Bookshop, Wenche Ommundsen, Sneja Gunew, and Debbie Golvan.

Thanks also to: Ivor Indyk, Robin Freeman, Ron Goodrich, Aaron Spelling, Angela and Yip Cho, Tara Phillips, Liam Phillips, Jules Wilkinson, Michelle Douglas, Hares and Hyenas Bookshop, Footscray Community Arts Centre (especially Bernadette Fitzgerald), Tseen Khoo, Jennifer Nation, Alison Goodman, Paul Byron, Owen Leong, Carly Patterson, Amadeo Marquez-Perez, Hayden Golder, Jacqueline Erasmus, Aperture Studios, Janette Hoe, Jennifer Anne Lee, Sophie Cunningham, Stephanie Holt, Michelle Bakar, National Young Writers' Festival, Kerry Watson, Christine McKenzie, Judith Rodriguez, Rosemary O'Shea, and everyone who came to hear me perform my work.

Most of all: my love and gratitude to my mother.

Influenced by the teen book series *Sweet Valley High*, TOM CHO began writing creative works in his mid-teens. He has a PhD in Professional Writing from Deakin University in Australia and, alongside his work as a fiction writer, he has a parallel career as a freelance writer and editor. Like his favorite pop stars, Tom enjoys trying new guises on for size, and his work has been described as being "transgenre, transgender, and transcultural all at once." His fiction has appeared widely, including in such publications as *The Best Australian Stories* series, *Asia Literary Review* and *The New Quarterly*. He has also performed his work on the stages of many festivals, from Singapore Writers Festival to Sydney Mardi Gras, and even at a Chinatown bar where he toured *Hello Kitty*, an award-winning show that combined literature with karaoke.

Born and raised in Australia, Tom is a newcomer to North America. He is currently writing a novel about the meaning of life. ***tomcho.com***